DAUGHTER
OF THE
WHITE ROSE

DAUGHTER
OF THE
WHITE ROSE

DIANE ZAHLER

HOLIDAY HOUSE • NEW YORK

Library of Congress Cataloging-in-Publication Data

Names: Zahler, Diane, author.
Title: Daughter of the White Rose / Diane Zahler.
Description: First edition. | New York : Holiday House, [2021]
Audience: Ages 8–12. | Audience: Grades 4–6. | Summary: In fifteenth-century
England, commoner Nell and her best friend since infancy, Prince Ned,
the future king, try to escape after being wrongfully imprisoned in the
Tower of London. Includes historical notes and timeline.
Identifiers: LCCN 2020012249 (print) | LCCN 2020012250 (ebook)
ISBN 9780823446070 (hardcover) | ISBN 9780823448975 (epub)
Subjects: LCSH: Great Britain—History—Edward IV, 1461-1485—Juvenile
fiction. | Great Britain—History—Richard III, 1483-1485—Juvenile
fiction. | CYAC: Great Britain—History—Edward IV, 1461-1485—Fiction.
Great Britain—History—Richard III, 1483-1485—Fiction.
Princes—Fiction. | Social classes—Fiction.
False imprisonment—Fiction.
Classification: LCC PZ7.Z246 Dau 2021 (print) | LCC PZ7.Z246 (ebook)
DDC [Fic]—dc23
LC record available at https://lccn.loc.gov/2020012249
LC ebook record available at https://lccn.loc.gov/2020012250
ISBN: 978-0-8234-4607-0 (hardcover)

FOR PHIL
YOU TOLD ME SO

FOR JULIUS
I WILL MISS YOU EVERYDAY

SEPTEMBER 1485

There is a riddle that Master Thaddeus told me, the last time I saw him.

We were in a tavern in Gravesend, and I was on the run for my life. Soldiers with swords had pursued me across the broad mouth of the Thames. They would kill me if they found me. They would kill Master Thaddeus, too, if we were seen together. But he had been the queen's fool, and riddling was his trade; he could not help himself. So he winked an eye and said to me:

> "The twin of a prince, but with no royal kin;
> A witness to murder, though no blood was shed;
> She once saved two kings, through both courage and fear,
> And one still lives on, but the other is dead.
> Who is she?"

I knew the answer, of course.

That twin, that witness, that brave, frightened girl was me. Me, Nell Gould, who once kissed a king, and rescued a prince.

Who was responsible for the death of the boy she loved more than any other.

Me, Nell Gould, who was the daughter of the queen of England's butcher.

This is how it happened.

CHAPTER ONE

"Papa, tell me my story!" I begged.

It was my fourth birthday, and I sat on my father's knee before the fire. I loved to hear the story of my birth, and of how Papa became butcher to the queen. The two tales were woven together like the threads of a tapestry, and I made him tell them again and again.

"Your story, Nell?" he teased me. "It is not yours, but the prince's story."

"Tell it!" I demanded. And Papa, who could deny me nothing, began.

In the year I was born, there were two kings in England.

One was King Henry the Sixth from the House of Lancaster, the house of the red rose. He was ill in mind and body; he had spent one entire year without speaking or moving, and he couldn't even drink without attendants' help. He was not esteemed, for he was a poor king, wasting English money on hopeless wars and giving other men's land to his favorites.

The other was King Edward the Fourth from the House of York, the house of the white rose. He was a distant cousin of King Henry's who had taken the throne by force of arms when Henry became too sick to rule. All the people loved King Edward—he was tall, handsome, gallant. He brought back order and peace, and his subjects were grateful for it.

But Henry grew better, and he wanted to win back his crown. So the two kings went to war, red rose against white, in the Wars of the Roses.

At that time, my mother was in her seventh month of pregnancy—and so was King Edward's wife, Queen Elizabeth. Of course, the queen could not go to war with her husband, but she couldn't remain in the royal palace, either; if King Henry's soldiers should get to her and take her, she would be in terrible danger. So, to stay safe, she went into sanctuary at Westminster Abbey, where none could be harmed, being under the protection of the church.

The abbey was at the end of our street. My father told me how he watched the procession of the queen and her attendants pass the house.

"Imagine it, Nell," he said to me, as I sat breathless on his lap. "All the merchants of King Street—the tailor, the saddler, the cooper, the fletcher, both of the bakers—standing outside their shops, with all their wives and children and servants. No one made a sound. We just waited. And then, at last, we saw the ladies coming, a long line of them in their silks and satins, walking down the street. Servants carried the princesses, as little as they were. The queen rode in a covered litter embroidered with the royal arms, and as she passed, we all cheered for her courage."

As he spoke, I could see the procession as clear as a painting: the little princesses, the beautiful ladies in their bright gowns, the servants carrying bags and boxes, the curtains of the litter parting just a bit as the queen peeked out to see her cheering subjects.

The abbey was just beside Westminster Palace. Papa's shop was so close that he often supplied the royal kitchens with meat for feast days, and he recognized one of the palace cooks as he walked past. Stepping out from the crowd, Papa cried, "Master Keene, does the queen have need of food?"

My father was not a forward-speaking man, but he hated the idea that Queen Elizabeth, as heavy with child as his own wife, could be in danger. "I knew I spoke above myself, Nell," he said when he told that part of the story. "My heart nearly beat out of my chest, I was that afraid!" I laughed, for I thought then that my father was not afraid of anything.

The cook stopped and looked searchingly at Papa. "Butcher Gould, is it not?" he said. "Do you know what you ask, sir? If you send food to the queen, and her cause is lost . . ."

He did not need to finish. Papa knew what might happen to him if he supported King Edward's queen and King Henry won the throne back. It would be treason, and he could go to prison—or even lose his head. Still, he nodded to Master Keene.

The cook smiled. "I will find out what we need and send

word to you," he said, and the somber procession passed by and through the great gates of the abbey, where Abbot Mylling waited to care for the queen, her daughters, and all their many attendants, and where they would be safe, protected by law from any of King Henry's followers who might have wanted to harm them.

The queen even stayed in the abbot's own quarters, which were grand, with wall hangings and gold plate. So she did not really suffer, except with worry about her husband and her own future.

That night, a messenger arrived at our rooms above the butcher shop on King Street. He carried a note on thick royal parchment that Papa kept always afterward on his person.

The queen has need of half-a-beef and two muttons for each week of her seclusion.

The queen was asking Papa to bring meat to her—to help her survive in sanctuary! Forever after, Papa's cheeks reddened with pride when he spoke of this message—and when he wanted comfort or reassurance, he would put a hand on the leather pouch at his belt that held that scrap of paper marked with the royal crest.

But this work was dangerous, and soon enough the news came that King Edward had been forced into exile in Burgundy. King Henry returned to London, traveled the three miles to Westminster Palace, and took back the throne—still sickly, but well enough to appear in public. The queen, too pregnant now to move, stayed in sanctuary, and King Henry, a devout man, vowed he would not harm her.

But he made no such vow to her supporters, and Papa had to be very careful when he brought the queen her meat.

As the weeks went by, Papa delivered the meat himself each Thursday, and he reported to my mother—and later described to me—how life went on inside.

"There were thieves and criminals of all types just outside the abbey walls," he said. "Men whose faces were scarred from fighting. Men who'd be long gone with your purse before you even noticed it was missing! Some were hungry, and the meat I carried was a great temptation to them. They would reach out to me and grasp at my packages. More than once I had to use my stick to hold them off!" I imagined these men, greedy or pathetic or both, and shivered at Papa's bravery.

Leaving the alleys of the outer sanctuary district, which surrounded the abbey, Papa would pass through a gate into the hush of the abbey compound itself. There, quiet monks walked by, their lips moving in silent prayer, and the scent of boxwood and herbs took over from the stench of manure and the sweat of the crowds that lived just outside. Papa would stride to the abbey kitchens and leave his packages with the grateful cook, sometimes giving pointers on how best to prepare the week's cuts—the mutton is a bit tough and would benefit from extra stewing, he would say, or the beef is young and tender and should not be masked with a sauce.

Occasionally, the queen would call him to her and they would exchange a few words, as she had none of the usual amusements of court to entertain her and longed for news of the outside world. My mother eagerly awaited Papa's descriptions of these visits.

"The queen is very large, and very uncomfortable," he told her. "She sits on a cushioned couch with her feet up on an embroidered stool. She said to me, 'Butcher Gould, do your wife's feet swell? My feet did not swell with my daughters, but with this child, I can barely walk.'"

"What did you say to her?" My mother loved these stories. She was only nineteen, and I would be her first child. She found it wonderful to think that a queen, more than a decade older and with several children already, should complain of the same ailments as a simple butcher's wife.

"Well, all the ladies gasped at her immodesty, but the queen doesn't seem to hold with common manners. She speaks her mind. I told her that your feet were swollen to twice their usual size, but that I was sure your discomfort could not be as great as hers."

"John!" My mother began to laugh.

"She *is* the queen, my love," Papa said, laughing as well. "Should your suffering be equal to hers?"

Queen Elizabeth had a reputation as variable as her moods. She was cold-hearted and proud, people said, but she had a hot temper. Many despised her because she was a commoner, the daughter of a mere knight—and she'd been married before, a widow and the mother of two children already when she wed the king in secret. Had the king tried *openly* to marry a commoner, Papa said, there would have been an outcry so great as to be heard across the Channel in France.

But common or not, the queen's family, the Woodvilles, were rich and powerful, and rumors of betrayal, treason, and even murder swirled around them. Some actually believed the queen used witchcraft to enchant King Edward into marrying her, but in truth, I always thought that her face was enchantment enough. Even swollen with child and fearful for her very life, Papa reported, her high brow remained unlined, her eyes as blue as a tranquil sky, her hair a smooth sheet of shining gold.

In sanctuary, with Papa, she let down her guard. I think now that she must have been frightened and lonely, and so she welcomed the knowledge that a butcher's wife was also seven, then eight, then nine months along, sharing in the common aches and pains that went with the condition.

Often Papa brought back a vial of rosewater for Mama from the queen—"To bathe your tired brow," he quoted—or a dainty pastry. And as both their confinements neared, he carried home one day an embroidered coverlet for my cradle. True, a lady-in-waiting had stitched the design of blue-and-gold flowers and green leaves, but in the corner was an interwoven *E* and *R*, *Elizabeth Regina*, done by the queen's own hand. It was our household's foremost treasure.

Mama's labor started early one Wednesday, and when it came time for Papa to deliver his meats to the abbey on Thursday,

I still had not been born. Her pains were dreadful, and Papa grew alarmed. He took it on himself to ask the queen for help. Though she herself was feeling the first twinges of childbirth, she sent with Papa her own doctor, the Italian Dr. Serigo. Mama protested when the doctor entered her bedchamber, wanting only her midwife, not the unknown attentions of a stranger, but Papa soothed her.

"The queen, too, labors, my love," he said, "and yet she sends you her doctor. She fears for your long efforts and wishes to help you. You must let the doctor do his work."

As Papa described it, Mama at last closed her eyes, sighed, and gave up her long struggle to the Italian, who knew at once that the birth cord was wrapped dangerously around my neck, and did what had to be done to help us both.

And so I was born, slippery and squalling, into the hands of Dr. Serigo, the same hands that hours later would hold the prince named Edward, the king's first son.

Dr. Serigo took my father aside after the birth. "Your wife is very weak," he told Papa. "She has labored two full days and lost much blood. Keep her abed for a fortnight at least, and be sure that she does not lift or scrub any time soon." Papa grasped the doctor's hand and tried to give him money, for he had saved Mama's life. But Dr. Serigo would take nothing but a cup of wine, stroking my damp red cheek before he returned to the queen.

"'You are a special one, my girl,'" Papa said, imitating the doctor's voice for me. "'You will share a birthday with the heir of England—surely this is a sign of great things for you!'"

That night the abbey bells rang out, and soon all of Westminster—and then all of London, and then all of England—knew that a prince was born. A prince—and a butcher's daughter, as well. Oh, but I loved that part of the story! I pretended, as I sat with Papa's arms tight around me and his beard warm and scratchy against my cheek, that the bells had rung for me.

Not much later, Papa recounted, he came home in a state of great excitement. "Alice!" he cried to Mama as she lay, still pale and feverish, in a bed made up beside the hall fireplace. "The queen wants to see our Nell!"

Mama gasped. "But—why?"

Papa perched beside her on the bed. "Dr. Serigo boasted of how he saved you—and Nell—and how it was by the queen's generosity in sending him to you that little Nell is here at all—"

"Which is true," Mama interrupted mildly.

"Yes, yes, so it is," Papa agreed. "But Queen Elizabeth was so pleased by the story that she wants to see its result. I am to bring Nell to her tomorrow!"

A lively spark came into Mama's eyes, and she struggled upright to help our serving girl, Mathilda, bathe me and comb my few hairs and dress me in my embroidered christening robe.

On a bright December morning, Papa carried me down King Street and into the abbey. There, he was taken into the room where the queen held court, which he later described to me so precisely that I can see it still, if I should close my eyes.

At one end of the room, a fire blazed in a huge carved fireplace, and every wall was draped with thick woven tapestries.

The floor, he said, gleamed with painted tiles, each decorated with a scene of royalty at play—hunting, dancing, feasting. Ladies sat on benches cushioned with embroidered pillows. They sewed and chatted, sounding, Papa said, like a flock of pretty birds, with one crow in their midst: the queen's fool, Master Thaddeus. He was a slight man who told riddles and tales in a singsong voice. His jester's clothes of motley stripes and patches stood out among the ladies' silks and velvets.

Before the fire played the queen's three daughters: Elizabeth, called Bess, who was four; Mary, three years old; and Cecily, one, who toddled after a gilded ball her sisters rolled to her.

In the middle of everything, the queen sat in a carved wooden chair beside an elaborate cradle. She seemed fully recovered from the suffering of childbirth and was as beautiful as ever. Her high-waisted gown was of gold brocade, trimmed with ermine and embroidered with vivid blue flowers. On her head was a white gauze butterfly headdress, from which her golden hair peeked out at her forehead. Papa's hands shook at this vision so that he feared he would drop me, and he faltered as he came forward to present me.

"Her Christian name is Eleanor, Your Majesty," Papa told the queen. "We call her Nell."

"She has a well-shaped head," the queen observed, tracing my cheek with her long fingers. "But I think she will not be a beauty. Comely, perhaps, but not a beauty." My father, who already thought I was a beauty, just nodded politely. And I, following the movement of that graceful hand with my unfocused eyes, somehow managed to reach up and grab a finger, grasping it tightly.

"Already trying to impress her queen!" Master Thaddeus observed.

The queen smiled her enchanting smile, and her ladies-in-waiting cooed, and little Princess Bess clapped her hands and said, "Oh, Mother, let's see how Nell likes our Ned."

So, with my father looking on astonished, I was laid in the cradle beside Edward, the Prince of Wales and heir to the throne of England, four hours younger and even balder than I. We babies fussed and squealed until at last we fell asleep, warm and safe together in a royal cradle, while the battle between King Henry and King Edward, the battle for a kingdom and the prince's future, continued outside the abbey walls.

CHAPTER TWO

But the story didn't quite end there.

"*The king is coming! Make way for the king!*" voices shouted from the street one morning. Papa leapt from the bed and ran to the window; Mama grabbed me from the cradle and held me tight.

"Whatever has happened, John?" she asked, frightened. Papa shook his head.

"Master John!" we heard Mathilda call from downstairs. Papa pulled on his clothes and scrambled down the narrow stairs to the hall, where Mathilda stood in a state of wild excitement. It was a moment before she was calm enough to speak.

"It's the king—our King Edward!" she managed at last. "The king is coming into London! Oh, sir!"

Papa, Mama, and Mathilda watched from our rooms above the shop as a mob of shopkeepers, servants, and merchants coursed through the streets. They learned, from the shouts below, that King Edward and his troops had sailed back to

England without warning. There had been a battle at Barnet, north of London, and King Henry's army was all but defeated. King Henry had given himself up to King Edward and was imprisoned in the Tower of London.

Queen Elizabeth had already left sanctuary and returned to Westminster Palace by the time we heard this. King Edward and his men marched to London, and they paraded south to Westminster and then down King Street under the banner of the white rose.

Papa and the others who had supported them—and many of those who had not—let loose with their cries and cheers. It was the first time I saw the king, Papa said, for he held me high so I could view the procession, and I waved my little hands and squealed my huzzahs with the rest.

Bells rang, and people shouted, and the king waved and smiled at the head of a line of mounted soldiers, his handsome face turning this way and that, his armor glinting in the weak spring sunshine. But he rode fast, and it was clear to all that he longed to see his new son for the first time.

· • ·

The king did not rest long with his family, however, for the war was not truly finished.

There was a huge battle right after that, King Edward's soldiers against the last of King Henry's. The two armies came together on Easter morning, in a thick mist on a field near London. Not five hours later, two thousand men lay dead, and finally it was ended.

Papa and Mama and I were at St. Margaret's, our parish church, when the tidings came. "The door of the church burst open"—Papa told the tale when I was older—"and we rose up from the pews in fear. Ladies screamed. The priest trembled at the pulpit. We knew there had been a battle, but we had no idea who'd won. Were these Henry's men, victorious, come to punish King Edward's supporters? Would they run us through with their lances, put our heads on pikes?"

"Oh, Papa!" I cried, shivering in delicious terror, for I knew the answer.

"Don't frighten the child, John!" Mama said reprovingly.

"But no," Papa went on. "They were King Edward's, carrying the banner of the white rose, and they pushed the priest aside and shouted to the congregation, '*The rightful and righteous King Edward has won the day!*'"

The cries of joy that rose at the news, Papa said, seemed to ascend through the vaulted ceiling of St. Margaret's straight to Heaven. For years the strife between Henry and Edward had divided town from town, even brother from brother, emptying the kingdom's treasury and leaving the people to wonder if there would ever be peace. So the gladness felt in Westminster that day was echoed throughout the kingdom.

King Edward returned to London once more, his foes defeated, his power secure. Henry the Sixth was his prisoner, and the war was over. King Edward and his friend Lord Hastings, darkly bearded and small beside the king, marched in triumph with all their soldiers through the streets. Papa watched the grand procession, heralded by trumpets and gaily colored flags and banners. Mama remained at home with me, but out the window she could see the crowds, and the bonfires, and the minstrels and street mummers flocking down the Strand—the road along the River Thames between London and Westminster—in merry celebration.

Papa danced and sang with them all night, but in the morning when he came back to us, his face was grim.

"King Henry is dead," he told Mama as she stroked his aching head. "Poor sick Henry is dead, God rest his soul."

"But how?" Mama asked, appalled.

"He died in the Tower last night. Some say he was murdered."

"By . . . King Edward?" Mama whispered.

"I cannot believe our king would order such a thing," Papa said. "People say it was the king's brother Richard who did the deed, to clear a path to the throne. Even King Henry's staunchest supporters wouldn't question King Edward's right to rule if Henry were dead. But who's to know what really happened?" He shook his head. "I must go out again, my love. They will be bringing King Henry's body through the streets to St. Paul's Cathedral. Surely if King Edward were guilty of . . . were responsible for his death, he would not allow that."

Mama nodded, and Papa splashed cold water on his face and changed his ale-soaked shirt before he left to walk the two miles up the Strand to St. Paul's. He stood with a silent crowd as the body of King Henry was carried publicly through London to the cathedral. They laid him there with his face showing so everyone could believe him truly dead.

"*Murder!*" was whispered in the alleys and back ways of Westminster. But all of England was tired of war and nothing could be proved, so the charges of murder faded away. Now, though, I wonder. I think that the darkness of those whispers cast a shadow over King Edward, and his whole family, that they could never quite escape.

With King Edward's return to Westminster, our family was forgotten, it seemed. There was no need of Papa's services, nor of mine. When Queen Elizabeth had lived in sanctuary, every so often a messenger from her court had come to our door. The prince was colicky, and Queen Elizabeth declared that only my warm self beside her son would soothe him when he howled. With the neighbors peeping from their doors, Papa would carry me down the street to the abbey, and I would spend some hours kicking and cooing in Prince Ned's cradle, helping him to calm himself and sleep. But this no longer happened. Our lives became more like our neighbors' lives.

I think that Papa must have missed the excitement and danger of that time. Now he spent his days going to the cattle market in Smithfield, visiting his pastures at Tothill where he raised beef, or overseeing his slaughterhouse, while his apprentice, Simon, helped Mama mind the shop. Two days a week, Papa himself worked in the shop while Mama made candles or stuffed sausages. I slept in my cradle at Mama's side or, as the months passed, played on the shop floor, which Mama and Mathilda worked hard to keep spotless.

In November I had my first birthday. We were sitting in the

hall before a warm fire when a knock came at the shop door. Mathilda was hoping to see Thomas, the draper's son, who was courting her, and she clattered through the shop eagerly, adjusting her hair and the neckline of her gown.

But in a minute she was back in the hall, her face pink. "Master John," she gasped, "it's a messenger from the king."

Mama looked up from her sewing, startled, as Papa stood and said, "Show him in, Mathilda."

The messenger, a young page, was clearly disdainful at visiting a butcher's home. He kept his hat on, and held himself in a way that hinted he feared getting his fine clothes dirty in such a house. Speaking in a high, nasal voice, he said in a rush, "Butcher Gould, the king's steward sends you the greetings of King Edward and Queen Elizabeth this second day of November and wishes you joy on the anniversary of your daughter's birth."

"Oh!" Mama breathed.

The page ignored her and continued. "The steward desires you to know that the king is aware of your sacrifice and your aid to his queen in her time of greatest need. To express his thanks, you are invited to become part of Prince Edward's household, as butcher to the prince."

Papa was stunned, and Mama burst into tears of shock and confusion, while Mathilda, speechless for once, flapped her apron up and down helplessly.

"What does this mean?" Papa asked finally.

"If you should accept the post, you will serve the prince's household as they need you. You will oversee the purchase and distribution of meats for said household, which numbers seventy-three." The page's sour expression made clear his opinion of Papa's presence at court.

"Seventy-three!" Papa murmured. How many sides of beef and mutton would that be? And the royal family ate other meats as well—capon, venison, lamb, kid. Ordinarily there was little call for such exotic fare in Papa's business. He would have to learn a whole new aspect of his trade.

"As befits a member of the prince's household," the page went on, "your rooms here on King Street shall be enlarged and a new sign provided for your shop. However, as your time will be spent for the most part at court, you will have to give over the daily business of your shop to your apprentices or journeyman."

"Of course," Papa said limply. "Well. Please tell His Grace that we are honored at the appointment. When does he wish me to begin?" There was, of course, no choice in the matter for Papa. It was a privilege he had to accept.

"Immediately." The page turned smartly and went to the hall door. He waited impatiently while Mathilda gathered her wits enough to open the door for him, and after his exit, Mama, Papa, and Mathilda sat in silence before the fire, too surprised to speak.

"It *is* an honor," Papa said at last. "And we won't be moving. We can keep the shop, and our home."

"We won't see you much," Mama said mournfully. "Meat for seventy-three! Do you think they'll give you an assistant?"

· • ·

In fact, they gave Papa three assistants. He had to provide enough for seventy-three hungry mouths daily, and he had to oversee the butchering and trimming of their meat, to ensure that all was of the very finest, freshest quality. It was an enormous responsibility. Even with his new helpers he worked day and night, for the Christmas season was coming on, with its many festivals and banquets.

Often he took me with him to the palace, for Mama was frequently ill in the cold months. The first time he brought me, one of the queen's grand ladies-in-waiting instructed him to take me up to the nursery, fearing that the heat and dangers of the kitchens with their five enormous fireplaces might harm me.

We were met at the door by Lady Mistress Darcy, the dour-faced woman who ruled the nursery. She glared at me, her expression darkening as she looked me up and down, from my not-entirely-clean dress to my scuffed leather shoes. I can clearly recall the way that, when she scowled, her long nose and even longer chin would nearly meet. She pursed her mouth and said, "This is the royal nursery, not a place to foster common orphans."

Father was furious. "She is not an orphan, Mistress. This is Eleanor Gould, who was born on the same day as the prince and delivered by the queen's own physician. Lady Woodville told me to bring her here."

Lady Mistress Darcy could hardly argue with that. Lady Woodville was not only a lady-in-waiting but the queen's sister, and no one to trifle with.

She allowed me to stay, but did her best to ignore me, and I her. The princesses, on the other hand, loved to play with me. I was like a doll to Bess and Mary. They could baby me in a way they could not treat their brother, who would be king someday. And Cecily, who was closest to me in age, became my friend.

I spent many a long winter day that year and for several more in the Prince of Wales's nursery. We were mostly overseen by his nurse, a sweet woman with a large, soft bosom who was given to great hugs and sudden kisses. I never knew her name. She was just Nurse, and she was nearly as kind to me as she was to her royal charges.

We had the finest tops and marbles, poppet dolls and stilts to play with, though just running through the privy halls of the palace and sliding on the smooth oak floors was a great game for us. Whenever we could escape the sharp eyes of Lady Mistress Darcy, we would explore the grand rooms and buildings of the palace: the Painted Chamber, with its biblical murals and grand canopied bed, where the king sometimes slept; St. Stephen's Chapel, with windows of glittering stained glass, its ceiling dark blue and scattered with gold stars; the King's Library, lined with oak shelves that held illustrated books in strange languages; the Jewel Tower, where the king kept his silver and jewels, and where we children were kept out by a dank-smelling moat.

But my favorite room was the Great Hall, where King Edward presided over celebrations and banquets. It was an enormous space with a beautifully carved and painted wooden ceiling, tall windows, and a huge marble table set at one end. The hall could hold hundreds of revelers, and often it did. Above its main floor was a long gallery, a balcony lined with portraits of royal relatives.

There, Princess Bess found a spot where we could spy on the performances and dancing below. Lady Mistress Darcy allowed it, as long as we were quiet; it kept us out of trouble. Night after night we would sit, Cecily, Mary, Bess, Ned, and I, breathless with the splendor and gaiety we saw beneath us.

Often the princesses would dance together in the gallery, mimicking the dances they saw below: the lively branle, the galliard, the slow and dramatic basse danse. Ned and I would talk then, peering down over the railing. He liked to watch his father preside over his courtiers, always in control of the festivities. King Edward was the biggest eater and drinker, the first on the dance floor, the most gallant to the ladies.

"How can he do all that?" Ned marveled on one of those magical candlelit nights. "How can *I* do all that when I'm king—and rule the kingdom too?"

I couldn't imagine Ned eating and drinking, dancing and fighting the way his father did. Though he looked like King Edward, with the same golden hair and blue eyes, the same stubborn chin, I didn't think they were really much alike. The king was large and loud and merry, and though Ned loved to have fun, he was often quiet and lost in his thoughts.

"You'll be a good king," I said, uncertain how to reassure him.

"That isn't enough," Ned said, staring downward as the king bowed to his partner in the carole. "I wish I didn't have to do it."

"Be king?"

He nodded, and I squeezed his hand in sympathy. That was like me wishing I could grow up to be a princess. I did wish it, all the time, but that didn't make it possible.

I can still remember a banquet we watched one St. Valentine's Day when I was perhaps five years old—or do I truly recall it? Perhaps it was my father's account of it, from his own vantage point in the hallway that led from the kitchens, that has kept it so vivid to me.

The Great Hall was decorated with wreaths of rosemary and bay, and their spicy fragrance rose up to us in the gallery. Love lanterns—silver and gold candleholders with cutout patterns—were scattered about. The tables were crowded with dishes so wonderful and rare that I had never seen most of them before. Each course had its own entertainment. Roasted salmon in an onion sauce, with a juggler who threw his balls so high that we could nearly catch them from the gallery. Rice with fruits, accompanied by minstrels' songs. Sliced, rolled chicken, and acrobats to go with it. Small crullers in the shape of hearts, with dancers leaping joyously.

In the center of the royal table was an edible illusion: a whole peacock, cooked and then refeathered, its mouth stuffed with cloth that was set ablaze so the bird seemed to breathe fire like a dragon. When the servers carried it out, everyone gasped and applauded, and up in the gallery we cried out in delight, quickly hushing each other so we would not be discovered. "Hours and hours, that bird took the poor cooks," Papa reported. "They had to re-place every single feather!"

After dinner, at one end of the room a large group of musicians played. Before them, the lords and ladies danced an intricate set, the ladies like a flock of peacocks themselves in their brilliantly colored gowns, the men fine in ermine-trimmed doublets and soft dyed leather shoes with points almost too long for dancing.

As we watched, I saw King Edward rise from his banquet seat on the raised dais, standing head and shoulders taller than the other men. His great laugh rang out, and he extended a hand to his queen. The minstrels struck up a basse danse, and the king and queen danced with wondrous grace, pausing between movements to exchange a Valentine's kiss.

There was one moment of that evening that I know for certain was my own memory, though I tried to forget it then and ever after. As the dance neared its end, I spied a man standing in a corner of the room. He was not someone I had noticed before; his hair was dark, his face pale, and he was the only one in that crowd of lords and ladies who did not smile. He stood watching and, it seemed to me, waiting for something. "Who is that man?" I asked Ned, pointing.

"My uncle Richard. He's come down from York to stay with us for a time," Ned told me carelessly.

"Richard? The Duke of Gloucester?"

"Yes."

"Why does he look so angry?"

"He isn't really angry. He always looks like that."

I watched him leave, and noted how he stood out among the happy, flushed figures around him. His clothes were drab, his features were sharp, and his look was cold. I shivered as he moved away. He cast a pall for me over the shimmering memory of that evening, and I resolved to stay clear of him.

But it was not to be.

A few months later, the gallery got us into trouble. Again we were watching the feasting down below, but there was only a single minstrel that evening, and no dancing, so we soon grew bored. Princess Cecily and I began tossing a leather ball between us, but one of my tosses went too high and plunged over the gallery railing to the tables below.

We heard a crash and a shriek, and the minstrel's song stopped mid-stanza. Ned and I froze in terror as Cecily, Mary, and Bess fled for the safety of the nursery.

Ned took my hand, and we walked to the railing. On tiptoe, we could just see over it. Down below, our ball balanced between the drumsticks of a stuffed chicken, next to the jug of wine it had overturned on the bounce. A furious lady-in-waiting, her yellow dress wine-stained, glared up at us. Next to her Lord Hastings, the king's dear friend, dabbed at her bodice with a linen cloth. In the doorway I could see my father, his face pale. I remember he told me that he was afraid for his position that night, and I well recall my own dread when King Edward looked up at us. He was frowning, and I trembled with fear.

"Come down here, children," he called up to us, and we stumbled down the stairs into the hall. Still clutching Ned's hand, I followed him to stand before his father. On one side of the king sat Queen Elizabeth, and on his other side was Ned's uncle Richard, Duke of Gloucester, with his narrowed eyes and grim expression.

"You've spoiled Lady Margaret's dress," King Edward said sternly.

"I'm sorry, Father," Ned said.

I snuck a look at him. He was standing straight and didn't seem to be afraid, so I straightened up myself and looked right at the king. Something came over me, and before I could stop myself, I curtsied deeply, a skill I'd learned from Princess Bess.

"I threw the ball, Your Majesty," I told him. "If it please Your Grace, you should blame me, not the prince."

The royal fool, Master Thaddeus, suddenly sprang out from beneath the table. I gave a little shriek. "Off with the girl's head!" he cried in his high-pitched voice. " 'Tis a capital offense, to have fun at the king's table!"

The ladies tittered, and for a moment the king's face didn't change. Then he threw his head back and roared with laughter, and his courtiers followed suit—all but Richard of Gloucester, whose brooding gaze rested on me for an unnerving moment.

"A fine throw it was, lass!" the king said. "Who is this minx who has dared to spill the king's wine?"

One of the queen's ladies looked up disinterestedly and said, "She's a butcher's child. Just a common girl."

"She should be punished," Richard of Gloucester said in a severe voice, taking a sip of his wine. "She has disrupted the king's dinner."

I froze, alarmed but determined not to show my fear.

Queen Elizabeth frowned. "This is the girl whose father supplied meats during our time in sanctuary, husband," she said to the king. "She was born on the same day as our son. She has been spending time in the nursery with the children."

The king raised an eyebrow. "A commoner playing with our children?" I wanted to sink through the floor, but kept straight and silent.

The queen didn't answer; she just looked at him. There must have been a great power in her gaze, for the king shook his head, smiling, then turned his piercing blue eyes on me. "Well done by your father, girl!" he said. "But try not to undo his work by tossing toys onto his fine meats." I curtsied again, certain that I would die of embarrassment.

"For a common girl, her throwing arm is most uncommon!" the fool exclaimed. He bowed deeply to me, the bells on the points of his cap jingling. Though his strange, leathery face was twisted in a half smile, half frown, his green eyes, as they met mine, were kind.

He turned back to the table and said, in a confidential tone, "The girl's run afoul of a fowl!" Then, when the courtiers laughed, he picked up the ball from where it rested atop the chicken and grabbed two hard-boiled eggs from a platter, tossing all three into the air and juggling them deftly. Even the queen looked amused at this, and King Edward waved us away, chuckling. We fled back up the stairs.

"The fool saved me!" I panted as we reached the safety of the gallery.

"That's Master Thaddeus," Ned said. "He'll do that—if any of us is in trouble, he can distract Mother and Father so they don't mind. He can say most anything, even to them."

"But who is he? I mean, who is he *really*?" I had seen him dozens of times but never thought to ask about him.

"He was a scholar once, at Oxford. But he got into trouble for his jesting there, and somehow ended up at court. He made Father so angry that he was banished to France, and then he made the king of France so angry that he was banished back here."

I was wide-eyed at the idea of being banished by two kings.

"So now he is Mother's fool. He follows her everywhere. Sometimes, when she is mad at Father, Master Thaddeus will even stand up for her against him. I think he's not afraid of anything."

I peered over the railing again to see this astonishing creature, but the fool had disappeared from view, and I soon forgot him as we went back to the nursery to play.

What I did not forget was Richard of Gloucester's insistence I be punished—the cruelty of it, the coldness, frightened me. After that, I hid when I saw him in the halls, but he took up residence in my nightmares, and I couldn't make him leave.

The day after the incident with the ball, Cecily ran to me when I entered the nursery. "Mother came this morning to talk to Lady Mistress Darcy about you!" she told me, breathless. "Don't worry, it's nothing bad. Only she wants you to have lessons with us!"

I looked to Lady Mistress Darcy to confirm this, and she nodded with her customary frown. "Obviously the queen feels you need some instruction in manners," she said drily.

I wasn't offended, though. How exciting, to have lessons with the princesses!

By the queen's orders, I was taught along with the others the right way to walk and stand, the correct use of table utensils, the proper forms of address for earls and dukes. We learned the simplest of dance steps. Cecily, Mary, and I had singing lessons, too, though my voice was so crowlike that often our lessons would end with Cecily and Mary convulsed in laughter. I even learned to recognize a few letters when the princesses' tutor came to instruct them in reading and writing English.

Ned began to have lessons of his own around then, but much of our time was still spent together. Though he was often quiet and solemn, with me he rarely seemed sad. He teased me mercilessly, dipping the ends of my hair in custard, or jumping out from behind a wall hanging to make me shriek, but he was sweet, too, letting me win at checkers and aiming me in hoodsman's blind so that I wouldn't knock over the supper tray and earn the wrath of Lady Mistress Darcy. Most of the prince's cuts and scrapes in those years he got chasing me through the halls of Westminster Palace. I think now that the royal household tolerated my presence because I *could* get Ned to laugh and play. Otherwise, he would have done nothing but look through books, or think his own grave thoughts.

We played outdoors, too; Ned was especially fond of the fishponds between the palace and the River Thames, where we could see enormous pikes churning the water as they waited to be caught for dinner. Mary felt sorry for them, trapped in the small ponds and destined for the kitchen ovens, but Cecily was both thrilled and terrified by them. "They have teeth!" she cried, backing away. "Fish aren't supposed to have teeth!" After that, of course, we had to pretend that we were going to push her into the pond, and she shrieked and struggled, loving the game.

We practiced archery too, sometimes with Lord Hastings's instruction. I was hopeless at it. But when my arrows would fall short, or bounce off the target, Lord Hastings was always kind to me. He would pat my shoulder, chuckle, and say, "Well, child, at least you are a better shot than Bess!" This was true; Bess had no strength in her arms at all and could barely pull the string back.

During the warmer months, the king's household moved from palace to palace about England, often stopping at the great homes of nobles, who spent all their money on feasts and entertainments for the huge royal retinue. When the king and queen went on progress like this, they would usually take Ned with them. Occasionally Papa would go as well to oversee the meat for the prince's household.

I was heartbroken then. I drove Mama to exhaustion and Mathilda to distraction with my whining and complaining, and I would sit in the shop door, blocking all who tried to enter, watching for a sign of the royal return. I gazed up the narrow, teeming, smelly street for hours, dreaming of Ned and the nursery, where the rooms were bright and sweetly scented and peaceful, even under the stern gaze of Lady Mistress Darcy.

Master Matthew, the mason, often passed me as he walked

down the street to Bell's Inn tavern. He would ruffle my hair and say, "So they've all left you and gone to Windsor, eh? Poor little orphan!" And he would laugh. I'd scowl at him, or, if Mama was not looking, stick out my tongue. I knew I was no poor little orphan; I was Eleanor Gould, daughter of the prince's butcher. But I missed my father when he was away, and I missed Princess Cecily, and most of all I missed my prince, missed our whispered secrets and our wild games, missed his serious blue eyes and the gold curls I liked to pull straight and release, marveling at how they always curled up again.

Still, the king and queen resided mostly at Westminster, so I passed my days in the bright whirl of palace life—until the summer that a new prince, Ned's brother, was born. In that season, everything changed.

CHAPTER THREE

I had begun to notice a difference in my mother. She was more often tired and couldn't play with me. She ate little, yet she grew plumper. Sometimes she was too weary to rise in the mornings and take her place in the shop. And when she *did* come to the shop, she would enter, look around at the bloody cuts of meat, take a deep breath, and run out again, her hand over her mouth.

I thought little about these events until, one day at the palace, we had word that Queen Elizabeth was to dine with her children. This didn't happen often, but when it did, I would be hurried away to the kitchen to take my midday meal with the cooks. It was not fitting that I should sit at the table with the queen.

In the frantic haste of preparations that day, though, I was forgotten. I made myself small and sat in a corner and watched. Nurse washed the children and combed their hair. Lady Mistress Darcy oversaw the setting of the nursery table and rattled off instructions to the nervous cook and servants.

Finally, Queen Elizabeth entered, Master Thaddeus close behind her. She kissed her children, taking Cecily onto her lap, and then noticed me in my corner.

"Come here, child," she commanded. I rose and went to her nervously. As I stood before her and dipped into a low curtsy, I was aware of how grubby I looked. Mama'd had no energy to wash me or comb my hair before I left. I felt ashamed.

"Nell, Nell, the butcher's daughter," the queen murmured. She smiled at me and I smiled uneasily back, glad when her attention turned to Princess Bess's new gown.

The servants brought in the meal. It was Friday, so there was a platter of fish, and I saw the queen blanch and cover her mouth. She suddenly stood and bolted from the room.

The fool danced about, mimicking the queen's movements, and we laughed.

"Mama does that," I remarked to Nurse, and she pulled me to her for a hug.

"Then soon you shall have a baby brother or sister, just as the prince will," Nurse told me.

I stared at her. "A baby?"

"Yes indeed," Nurse said. "When the smell of good fresh trout makes a lady ill, it's a sure sign that she is with child."

"Just you wait," Master Thaddeus said, crouching down. "She'll grow bigger and bigger and bigger still, and then she'll . . . pop!" And he leapt up like a devil-in-the-box, making us all scream.

"You!" Lady Mistress Darcy said fiercely, pointing at the fool. "Out!"

Feigning terror, Master Thaddeus slunk to the door. There he turned and said, "A riddle: What do you break if you so much as name it?"

We looked at each other, puzzled.

"Why, silence, of course, you babes and simpletons!" he cried, and ran out of the room.

Although the rest of the day was made miserable with Lady Mistress Darcy's fuming about the ruined dinner, I was as happy as I had ever been, imagining a baby to hold and spoil and play with, a living doll of my very own. Now I would not have to be lonely when Ned left with the court for a journey to another palace.

When Papa came for me that evening, I told him what had happened.

"Is it true?" I asked. "Will I have a new baby brother or sister?"

Papa sighed and held me close. "Aye," he said, without joy. "I do hope so." I thought this an oddly halfhearted response to such thrilling news, but I forgot it as soon as we arrived home and I could run to Mama.

"Really, Mama?" I asked her. "Are you going to have a baby?"

She held my hand over the swell of her belly. "Do you feel that, my love?" she asked. I felt the taut skin beneath her dress, and then something else, a light flutter under my hand.

"Oh!" I gasped. "Is it there? Inside?"

My mother laughed. "That's exactly right. Inside now, but it will be outside soon enough."

A baby! I was so excited that I hardly noticed the circles beneath my mother's eyes, or the way her voice quavered when she spoke of the child coming out.

How could I? I was so small, and mostly life was lovely for us then. Our house had grown grand since Papa's appointment to the prince's household. We had a hall, a buttery where we stored our food, and a kitchen. There was a large bedroom upstairs, with a ladder leading to the solar, a partitioned room under the peaked roof where Mathilda and Papa's apprentices slept. At the king's orders, a parlor had been built for us, too, and above it were added two more bedrooms, one just for me. This meant I had to sleep apart from Mama and Papa. I did not much like it, but I knew that they were just on the other side of the wall.

Our rooms were lavishly decorated. We had wall hangings of silk, and silver candlesticks. Our beds were new and stuffed with feathers, not straw, and we had warm coverings. The house was comfortable and welcoming, for we could afford to keep fires in all the rooms.

I took this luxury for granted. My father was the royal butcher, and I was friend to the Prince of Wales. I thought myself the luckiest and the best of girls.

It was hardly surprising that I had no friends on King Street. Many of the neighboring merchants also worked for the royal households, but their children didn't play with royalty as I did. I held a peculiar position among them. When I wished to, I could fascinate a crowd with tales of my adventures at the palace, but these same children made fun of my clothes and refused to let me join in their games. As Nick, the chandler's son, once said to me, "Ye're too good for the likes of us!"

"I'm not!" I protested, though of course I thought I was. "Let me play!"

"You'll dirty your dress," said Joan, the baker's daughter, her voice both mocking and envious. Without thinking, I smoothed the green silk of my hand-me-down skirt, which had once belonged to Princess Cecily, and the others laughed at me, turned away, and ran into a nearby alley to try to roll hoops in the dirt.

Sometimes I longed to play jacks or dolls in the gutter with Nick and Joan and their friends. I grew tired of trying to keep my clothes neat and my face clean on the chance that I might see the king or queen about the palace. And I was often lonely, especially in the summer when Ned was away. I would sit indoors with the windows open wide, listening to the sounds of other children laughing and shouting as they played tag up and down King Street and wishing I could join them. The few times that I did, though, they mocked me or tripped me as I ran or—worse—just ignored me.

As the months passed and I moved between the bustle of King Street and the splendor of Westminster Palace, I began to notice that the queen's pregnancy was progressing differently from my mother's. As the queen grew larger, she complained endlessly of the early summer heat, but she glowed with health. Her hair seemed even more lustrous, her skin luminous.

Mama, on the other hand, was always draped in warm shawls, despite the unusual spell of hot weather. Even then she sometimes asked Papa to rub her hands or feet to warm them. Her skin was pale, with a grayish cast, and though her stomach grew large, the rest of her seemed to dwindle, until sometimes she appeared to be all belly and sunken eyes. For much of the summer she lay abed, and I was instructed to play quietly by myself and not disturb her.

Because the queen was pregnant, the royal family stayed at home that summer. I escaped happily to the palace when I could, shedding the feelings of unease that I had at home when I entered the bustling royal nursery. Nurse took care of me in the ways Mama was no longer able to—making sure I ate my meals, combing the knots from my hair as I squirmed and complained, having my torn clothes mended or replaced as I outgrew them. I proudly wore the princesses' plainest castoffs—I could not take their velvets or cloth of gold, as it was against the law for commoners to dress above their station. I must have looked a sight in those days, parading down the street in my fine, oversized dresses, clutching the hand of Papa, who, more often than not, had forgotten to take off his apron streaked with dried blood and crusted with the entrails of a half dozen different animals.

Because the lords and ladies were all at Westminster, that

summer we saw our first jousts—astonishing spectacles that pitted knight against knight in the dusty meadows of Smithfield. The princesses, Ned, and I sat shaded in specially built stands, while below us the knights, sweltering in their metal shells, galloped toward each other at top speed, lances out. When one or the other went flying, or a lance splintered, we would scream ourselves hoarse cheering for the winner, though the loser was often carried off on a cloth stretcher, bloody and broken.

· ● ·

In mid-August, Mama's pains began. It was a hot, windless day. The smells from the shops that lined King Street—the bakery, the tannery, the brewery—mingled and hung in the air, thick and choking. William, our new apprentice, had to fan the meats constantly to keep the flies from landing.

Papa and I left early for the palace, while Mama was still able to smile and kiss me. Mathilda and the midwife stood by Mama's bed as I approached, and the atmosphere of the room, dim and stifling with the shutters closed to keep out the bad air, alarmed me.

"Don't worry, my Nell," Mama said, stroking my hair. "By the time you come home tonight, there'll be a baby to play with!" But then she turned away and groaned.

I didn't want to leave, but I was far too scared to insist on staying. Once at the palace, I wouldn't play with the others, and when Ned kept pestering me, I finally lashed out at him, pulling his hair and slapping his face so hard a red mark showed. I shudder now to think of it. To strike the Prince of Wales was a treasonous act. Even at such a tender age, it could have landed me in prison—or worse.

Ned said nothing, though, only stared at me with tears welling in his great blue eyes, and I burst into tears myself.

"My mama is crying and moaning," I sobbed. "I'm afraid she'll die."

"Oh, Nell," Ned whispered. Slap forgotten, he came to me and put his arms around me. When Nurse found us thus, red-eyed and runny-nosed, she pulled us both onto her lap.

"What ails you, poppets?" she asked, pushing my hair from my sweaty face.

"Nell is afraid for her mama," Ned told her, his brow furrowed.

"Oh, my little dear, your mama's just having her baby," she soothed me. "Ladies do groan and cry with it. It's hard work, and it hurts—worse than a cut finger. But they get through it. All mothers have done it, sweet Nell. Think of how many mothers have gone and had babies! Now, what about a seed cake?"

We ate the cake, but it didn't help much. The hours dragged by, the heat not lifting as darkness fell, and I wasn't surprised when Papa failed to come for me. It was a day when nothing could go right. At last I fell asleep in Ned's bed, and woke there in the first faint light of morning, still tired, hot, and sticky. Nurse was standing over me, her kind eyes shadowed.

"Get up, little one," she whispered. "Your papa's here to take you home."

I crawled out of bed, leaving Ned sleeping peacefully, and stumbled into the nursery. Papa sat there at the table, his head in his hands. I went to him and touched his arm, and the face he turned to me was terrible with grief. Helplessly, frightened beyond speech, I started to cry, and he held me close as I sobbed.

"Let's go home, Nell," he said at last. His voice was thick with weariness.

We made our way through the palace halls, stirring now with the first activity of the day, and slowly, hand in hand, back up King Street. We dodged the drinkers slumped outside Bell's Inn, ignored the greeting of Master Matthew, and at last reached our house, where my new brother howled in the able arms of a wet nurse and my mother lay dead of his birthing.

I remember little of the next few weeks. I know Mama was buried, but I don't think I witnessed the burial. I was lost in those days. I recall hearing that Queen Elizabeth had given birth to a son, a new prince called Dickon, and I can remember my bewilderment that Ned should keep both his mother and his brother, while I had a brother but a mother no longer.

My brother, Tobias, seemed at first to cry constantly. The nursery was next to my room, and Toby's wails would keep me awake, but I didn't want to go in and see him. The wet nurse had charge of him. Papa could not bear to hear the howls, so he was rarely at home. He didn't take me with him when he went to the palace, but I didn't mind. I didn't want to see anyone, not even Ned.

I wandered through our grand rooms like a wraith, searching for a sign of my mother—her scent on a chair cushion, or one of her long brown hairs on a bedroom coverlet. But I could not find her anywhere, and at last one day my wanderings took me to the nursery.

The wet nurse had just fed Toby, and he lay in the cradle drowsily, blowing little milk bubbles with his soft pink lips. As I moved uneasily through the doorway, his eyes found me, and he made a little "Eh-eh-eh" noise. To me, it sounded like "Nell-Nell-Nell," and I ran up to the cradle, amazed.

"Nell-Nell-Nell," Toby said again, waving his tiny fists wildly. His eyes were a deep grayish blue, like Mama's, and he had no eyebrows at all. I could hardly believe the perfection of this hairless, toothless baby. I looked deeply into his eyes, and it seemed to me I saw Mama looking back at me.

From that moment, I was Toby's completely.

Papa, too, eventually fell victim to baby Toby's charms. He could not long blame the babe for his mother's death; instead, he took comfort in Toby's sweet babbling and cries of hunger. Indeed, if I had not loved my brother so passionately, I would have been jealous of the attention my father gave him. But we were two lonely souls, Papa and I, and we turned to Toby to soothe us in our sorrow. Before a month was out, he had us both laughing at his wide, toothless grins—though they were only from gas, the wet nurse insisted.

· ● ·

When the leaves had begun to turn and the days got cool, Papa came to me as I played with Toby in the nursery. He looked solemn.

"Nell, you've been summoned to the palace tomorrow. The prince is leaving. He wants to bid you farewell."

"Leaving?" I said, tickling Toby's little fingers as he kicked in his cradle. "Where does he go this time?"

"He leaves for good this time, my dear. He is being sent to the Welsh Marches to learn to be a king."

I stared at Papa in bewilderment. Leaving, for good? That wasn't possible!

I started to cry and couldn't stop. I had lost so much; must I now lose my dearest friend? My desperate sobs unnerved Papa. I would not be soothed, and at last he asked Mathilda to put me to bed, where I wept half the night before I fell asleep.

In the morning, Mathilda dressed me in my best gown, and Father and I walked in a dreary autumn drizzle to the palace. We trudged up the great stone stairs to the nursery. There we found a scene of chaos and high emotion, with the princesses all weeping, Ned grim and silent, Nurse fluttering helplessly, the new baby howling with colic, and Lady Mistress Darcy issuing order after order and ignored by all.

I went straight to Ned and sat beside him at the nursery table. He took my hand and held it tightly. "Where have you been, Nell?" he asked, his face a mask of misery.

"I've had to mind my brother," I said. "I didn't know you had to leave."

"I don't want to go," he said wretchedly, "but Father says I must."

I nodded. "My papa says you must learn to be a king."

"How can I learn that?" he demanded. "I can't be a king, I can't! It's too hard!"

I knew that the prospect terrified him. He'd told me so during our evenings in the gallery. He couldn't imagine growing to be a man like his father, outsized and fierce and powerful. He hated the idea of war, hated the bewildering intrigues of court that we had so often watched unfold from our vantage point above the revelry.

"It will be a long time before you are king," I comforted him. "You have years and years to learn."

Ned saw the logic in that, and his brow smoothed, his panic easing a bit.

"Will you ever come back?" I asked him.

"My lady mother says I will come back sometimes—maybe for Christmas, or Michaelmas, and some other times as well. And she says you may visit with us then. But I shan't live with my family—never again!"

This seemed dreadful to me, but I knew there were things more dreadful. So I said, "At least your mother is still alive, and you can see her sometimes."

He hung his head for a moment and then looked at me. "I know. I'm sorry, Nell. Are you terribly sad?"

"Yes," I said simply, but I didn't cry. I had no more tears left in me. "I miss her all the time. I'll miss you all the time too."

We sat glumly on a pile of trunks in a corner of the room, watching as Ned's clothes and belongings were carried out to the wagons that would take them to Ludlow Castle, a freezing keep on the Welsh border. My heart ached for Ned. Though I had lost my mother, I still had my home and family. Ned was leaving both—and leaving behind his childhood, as well. There would be little time for games at Ludlow, we both knew, and few playmates.

At last the time came for leave-taking. Ned hugged me tightly and said, "I will write to you, Nell. And I will think of you every day."

"I'll think of you, too," I said. I was proud that my voice was steady.

He kissed his sisters and his new brother. Bess and Mary dissolved in tears, but Cecily came over and put an arm around me.

"He'll come back," she whispered. "And while he's away, you and I can play."

I nodded and squeezed her hand. Then the king and queen entered to take formal leave of their son. I didn't want to see them—I blamed them for sending Ned away. I ducked from the nursery and ran to a window that I knew overlooked the inner courtyard, where the prince's carriage waited for him.

Soon Ned emerged into the rain, holding the hand of his dour uncle, the queen's brother Lord Rivers, who was to accompany him and watch over him at Ludlow. "He is very kind," Cecily told me in a low voice, coming to join me, "but he doesn't care for music or dancing. Poor Ned!" They climbed into the closed carriage, and Ned leaned his head out the window for a last look at Westminster.

I cannot say what lucky chance made him look up, but he saw me at the window. He didn't wave or move at all, but his eyes held mine for a long moment. I recall as clear as day his unwavering gaze and the brave set of his mouth as the driver flicked the reins and the horses pulled my prince out of the courtyard and away from my life.

CHAPTER FOUR

With Ned gone, I threw myself into raising Toby. I rejoiced in his first real smile, rocked him as he howled while cutting his first tooth, changed him and washed him and played with him. I was only a child myself, but I had watched Nurse mind the royal children for years, and I did the same for my brother. I tried my best to be a mother to him.

Much of Ned's household had gone with him to Ludlow, so Papa became one of the king's butchers, with even more work to do at the palace. That left me with still greater responsibility at home. I went back to the royal nursery from time to time, but it began to seem uncomfortable and awkward. The princesses were learning poetry, and French, and manners for state dinners—skills that were useless to me. A distance was growing between us.

I asked Cecily about Ned during one of my visits, and she told me, "Uncle Rivers wrote to our lady mother that he was well. He spends a good deal of time reading and writing. It sounds dreadfully dull. It's all at Father's command, you know. He told Uncle Rivers not to let poor Ned have any fun at all."

"But the king loves to have fun!" I said. It was true; nobody enjoyed enjoying himself more than King Edward. He was always dancing, riding, playing chess and hazard and shovelboard.

"Bess told us that Father said Ned must study all morning, and practice at swords all afternoon, and go to bed at eight."

"Well, he won't mind the studying too much," I said. "But bed at eight!"

Cecily shook her head. "What else is there to do at Ludlow? No banquets, no jousts, no dances. It sounds very bleak—I'm glad *I* don't have to go!"

My heart sank as I pictured poor Ned in a dank stone castle with nothing for company but his books and the pious Lord Rivers. "Why would the king want that for Ned?" I asked.

Bess was eavesdropping, and she answered me. "He doesn't want Ned to be like him. He wants him to be better. Smarter. He wants him to be a great king."

"But—" I began. It had never occurred to me that King Edward was not the greatest of kings. Certainly that was what Papa believed. If the king wanted Ned to be still better . . . what did that mean? I looked to Bess for an answer, but I couldn't read the expression on her face. I decided to ask Ned about it when he came home.

But Queen Elizabeth was wrong about Ned's return, and he did not come back for Christmas, nor for Michaelmas the next fall, nor that Christmas either. I spoke of the prince less and less, except to Toby, who listened wide-eyed to my stories of the palace and the wonders I had witnessed there. On my few visits to see the princesses, I felt ever more out of place. Princess Bess was changing; she was older, taller, and disinclined even to speak to me, much less play with me. Soon, I knew, she would be betrothed to some prince or king, then married and sent away to be queen of a faraway country. She even had three ladies-in-waiting now, noble girls who looked me up and down with disdain. And Bess began to echo their scorn. Once, when I walked in, she looked pointedly at my untidy hair and said, "Really, Nell, couldn't you even brush your hair before visiting the royal palace? And your hem is torn. Whatever were you thinking?"

As her ladies tittered, Cecily, red-faced, cried, "Stop it! Nell is our *friend*, Bess!" She would have launched herself at her sister, but Lady Mistress Darcy stepped between them and sent Bess and her ladies to Bess's bedchamber.

Mary was kinder, and Cecily of course was always welcoming, but they chattered about the saltarello dance that a nobleman from Ferrera had taught Bess, or the shocking laced bodice that the Countess of Surrey had worn the week before, or the faceted sapphire rings they had all been given by a Spanish diplomat, and I felt quite left out. So gradually I stopped my visits altogether.

· ● ·

Before long Toby was walking and talking, a babbling whirlwind that I had to watch closely. He could get into trouble in less than an instant; I was kept busy righting overturned ewers and mopping up the messes, keeping him from the ever-beckoning fire, and wiping away tears after his frequent tumbles. I couldn't take him into Father's shop at all; with the knives and the entrails, he'd have been sliced to bits or soaked in sheep's blood before I could blink.

Sometimes we wandered the streets of Westminster, stopping to gaze in the windows and talk with the merchants. Now that I no longer went to the palace and had outgrown all my handed-down finery, Nick and Joan and the others would sometimes speak to me. They even invited me to join in their games once or twice, but somehow I no longer wanted to. Toby was glad to play with the littlest ones, though, and he quickly learned to keep up. I had to stay alert to keep him safe in the chaos that was King Street, but I loved to watch him, so tough and sweet and funny. He was my greatest joy.

The fall I turned nine, a messenger stopped by our house with a great surprise: a letter. We had never received a letter before; I hardly knew anyone who had. Of course, I could not read it. I had learned some English letters and words with the princesses at the palace, but not enough actually to read. I placed the message on the table, and Toby and I hovered over it anxiously until Papa came home.

"Da—look! Look what's here!" Toby cried in his piping voice, dancing round Papa in a frenzy of excitement.

"Let me take off my apron," Papa said, handing the stained garment to Mathilda. She took it with her usual grimace, holding it out at arm's length. "Settle down, boy! What is it?"

I handed him the letter.

"By the saints," Papa swore. "A letter. In Latin! With the royal insignia! It's addressed to you, my Nell."

"To me!" I could hardly believe it. "Oh Papa, can you read it?"

Papa had learned to read both English and Latin at the parish school where he grew up, and though he struggled with the words, he could make them out.

"'From His Grace Edward, Prince of Wales, to his most . . . most loyal subject and good friend Eleanor Gould, greetings.'" He paused to take a breath.

"Go on!" I begged.

"There's not much more. 'I am practicing my writing. I shall write again. I hope you are well. Good-bye.' Then it's signed with the prince's signature." He handed the letter to me, and I gazed at it, deeply impressed.

"What word is *friend*?" I asked.

"Here. *Amico.*" Papa pointed. I stared hard at the markings on the thick, creamy parchment. The Latin looked like the scratchings that the chickens made in the dirt of our courtyard. It seemed impossible that anyone could find words in them.

I followed Papa into his room, where he splashed water from a pitcher into a bowl and began to wash off the day's blood and grime.

"Papa," I said hesitantly, turning the letter over and over in my hands. "Do you think that I could learn to read and write Latin?" I knew that noble girls sometimes did. Though there were no schools for them, they could be tutored. I didn't really see why I couldn't have a tutor too.

Papa dried his face and hands briskly. "You want to learn Latin, eh?" he asked me, emerging from his towel. "Is it so you can send letters back and forth to Ludlow?"

"Well . . . yes."

"Oh, Nell. Come here, my girl." Papa sat heavily on the bed, and I came to stand in front of him. "Prince Ned will be king one day, you know. He'll be King Edward the Fifth."

"I know."

"He cannot be friends with you forever. It wouldn't be . . . seemly. You are only the daughter of a butcher."

"But you are the king's butcher!" I protested, offended at the word *only*.

"Yes, one of them," Papa allowed. "But just a butcher nonetheless. You are not the prince's equal. You know that, don't you?"

I looked at my feet, distressed. I did know it, in a way. I knew we were commoners, though now rather wealthy ones. We weren't the social equals of the lords and ladies, the earls and dukes who surrounded the king, much less of the royal family.

Yet when Ned and I played and talked together, there seemed to be no barriers between us. I believed that, in some way, we *were* equals. And I felt that knowing this language he wrote in would bring us even closer.

But I could never say such a thing to Papa.

"I know," I told him instead. "But he's very lonesome at Ludlow. I think a letter from me would cheer him."

Papa shook his head. "What use would learning Latin be to you? I cannot allow it, Nell. He is gone from us. You must face that."

My lip trembled, and he sighed.

"I'm sorry, love," he said gently. "You should learn your English letters and your numbers, that is true. It would be a useful study for you, so you're able to manage your household when you marry—even to do your husband's accounts, should he want you to. But Latin . . . you would need special schooling for that. For Toby to go to school, there is some reason. He may lead the guild someday. But you'll marry and have children. What need have you for Latin?"

I hated it when Papa spoke to me of marriage. The boys I knew on King Street were all helpless, hapless creatures. I could no more imagine marrying one of them than I could see myself dancing a galliard with the king of France. Marry Ralf Lydgate, the cooper's son, with his greasy hair and always-running nose? Or Hugh, the mason's son, who bullied younger children and stole from every shopkeeper who turned his back? But I knew Papa spoke sense. No girls on King Street could read or write Latin. Even the milliner, Mistress Bennet, who was a widow and ran her business alone, could barely read and write in English.

There was no need for me to learn Latin—but what I *wanted* was a different matter entirely.

From then on, I looked at the three books in our oak cabinet with a new eye. They were bound manuscripts, painstakingly handwritten and beautifully illustrated. Papa had been given them as gifts by the king's Master of the Household, and he considered them a great treasure. There was a Latin collection of psalms decorated in blue and gilt; a wonderful tale in English called *Tristrem and Lancelot* that he'd read to us so often we'd memorized it; and a Latin commentary on the *Song of Songs*, which had lovely pictures. I had often thumbed carefully through these volumes, looking at the bright paintings of angels and knights. Now I longed to know what the words inside them said.

But since Papa would not change his mind, I took matters into my own hands.

One afternoon, I went to the abbey to visit the grammar school there. It was in a small room to the side of the main chapel. I had often peeked in through the door to admire the wall painting of a white hart, the tall shelves of books, the carved wooden tables and chairs where students studied, but I'd never been inside. I stood outside the room a long time, gathering my nerve and listening to the boyish voices chanting in Latin. Then I took a deep breath and pushed open the door.

Twenty-eight voices broke off as twenty-eight faces turned to stare at me. No, twenty-nine, for the schoolmaster—a tall, lanky man with pockmarked skin—stared as well. I stood my ground, trembling, breathing in the smells of dust and leather-bound books and sweat.

"If you seek the almonry, girl, it is next door," the schoolmaster said. A boy tittered.

"No sir," I replied, annoyed at the suggestion that I was looking for alms. I was no beggar! "Are you Master Fuller?"

He frowned. "I am."

"Then it is you I would speak with," I said bravely. "I want to learn to read and write."

There was dead silence for a moment, and then a roar of laughter went up from the boys. I looked at them and saw row upon row of unfriendly, mocking faces—faces of little boys, of boys my age, of boys nearly grown to men. My cheeks flamed red with embarrassment, but with anger too. How dare they laugh at me?

"*Quiet!*" Master Fuller shouted, grabbing a switch from a hook on the wall and waving it. The laughter stopped as abruptly as the ending of a thunderclap.

Master Fuller strode to where I stood, and I sank my nails into my palms to keep my eyes dry and my breathing steady.

"You are a girl," Master Fuller informed me. An unrestrained snicker broke out, and the master raised his switch again. "Girls do not go to school," he continued. "What need have you of Latin grammar? Learn to cook and run a household, child. If your mind needs exercise, take up embroidery, or play the psaltery. Those are pursuits that enhance womanly appeal. No man wants a wife who is more educated than he."

With that, I was dismissed. Master Fuller turned his back on me and instructed the boys to begin their chants again, and I ran through the door humiliated, followed by the piping strains of Latin recitation.

When Papa came home that night, he noticed the traces of

tears on my face, and without much effort got the whole story from me. He was upset that I'd disobeyed him, but angrier at the schoolmaster's treatment.

"Fuller is a fool!" he said heatedly. "Who is he to say my girl cannot learn? You are as smart as—smarter than—any of his schoolboys!" With joy, I saw that my actions had done what my words could not—changed Papa's mind. But he still would not send me to school. He had a different plan.

A few evenings later, Papa invited someone home to dine.

"He is Master Caxton, a printer," Papa told me that morning. "We were boys together in Canterbury, before I was apprenticed in Westminster and he in London. I believe he may be willing to teach you, so try to appear levelheaded when you meet him." He smiled to show he was only teasing.

"Teach me!" I cried. "Teach me to read?"

"In English. If he thinks you are worthy," Papa said. It wasn't all that I wanted, but it was good enough for now.

We rarely entertained, so we were in an uproar to ready ourselves for the visitor. The house was swept and polished, and the table at the raised end of the hall was set with our best plate. A crackling fire burned in the hall's hooded fireplace, as the late autumn weather had turned cold, and in the parlor, wine was ready in pewter goblets. Papa even hired Mag Howell, a widow who lived in one of the alleys off King Street, to cook the meal. I wore my best gown—the only one unstained, as Mathilda was unreliable with the washing.

Master Caxton arrived as the abbey bells were ringing for

Vespers. I curtsied to him as gracefully as I could. He bowed in return and said, "Honored to make your acquaintance, Mistress Nell."

Immediately I liked this short, round man with his long beard and red velvet cap. I knew he was very distinguished—Papa called him the king's printer—but he took the trouble to put me at my ease and make me feel comfortable.

I left Master Caxton and Papa alone in the parlor for an hour, but Toby and I joined them when it came time to dine. We ate a veritable feast: pastries with beef marrow, grilled bream in verjuice, Papa's best roast. Mathilda served us in a frenzy of nerves, muttering under her breath as the wine sloshed from the pitcher and the roast slipped off its plate, nearly ending up in Master Caxton's lap. He steadied her arm gently, and was as polite to her as if she had been mistress of the house and not a servant. He ate heartily, complimented the food and our home, teased little Toby, and entertained us with stories of his travels to the Low Countries.

"Bruges is all canals," he told us. "Think of that! The people there use boats to get from place to place. Imagine taking a boat to church or the markets!"

"Is it very beautiful?" I asked, picturing a town where water lapped at every doorstep.

"Much of the time, it is," Master Caxton said. "In springtime, the canals are filled with mother swans swimming with their cygnets, and flowers float among the boats. In winter, the water freezes white, and Flemish burghers skate from shop to shop, wrapped in furs. In the heat of summer, though, the stink from those canals could *choke* you!" Toby giggled, but I was enthralled, imagining such a faraway, magical place.

After dinner, Toby went to bed, and we sat before the fire. Papa poured our guest spiced wine, and Master Caxton stretched his legs out and folded his hands over his plump stomach.

"Now, Mistress Nell, we must get down to business. I've heard that you want to read and write."

"Yes, sir," I said nervously. Had I made a good enough impression? Would this important man agree to teach me?

"Here." Master Caxton rose and took a poker from its hook beside the fire. He traced a mark in the ashes on the hearth. "Do you know what this is?"

"No, sir," I admitted, ashamed. I knew it was a letter, but I couldn't remember which one.

"No, of course you don't. It is an *A*. The first letter of our English alphabet, from which all our words are made." He handed me the poker, and I painstakingly copied the mark he had made.

"*A*," I said.

"That's very good!" he exclaimed. "See, you have mastered *A* already. Now there are only twenty-five more letters for you to learn." We repeated the exercise with *B* and *C*, and when I was done Master Caxton looked very pleased. "I believe we could have you reading in a matter of months, my dear."

"You'll teach me?" I could hardly believe it. "Oh, sir, thank you! Thank you!"

"Why don't you come to my shop . . . let us say . . . thrice weekly, at midday. We'll have a lesson, and then you can help in the shop for a time. Does that meet with your approval, John?" he asked my father.

"You must study hard, Nell, and try to be a help and not a hindrance," Papa said sternly, but his eyes twinkled above his beard.

I would learn to read!

· • ·

I went to Master Caxton's shop the following Monday. It was near the abbey, beside the almonry. Hanging above the door was a small sign marked with initials that I later learned were Caxton's own, and above that was a larger sign showing a shield with a red pale, a red stripe between two white stripes. I knew Master Caxton was not a nobleman, so he would not have a coat of arms himself. It must, I decided, belong to whatever lord had rented the shop to the printer.

I entered nervously and looked around me. The room I was in had high ceilings and an enormous piece of wooden and metal machinery at its center. A window with leaded panes made the space bright, and beneath the window was a long table holding wooden stands on which open books rested. Drawn by the books, I started toward them, but a boy of perhaps ten or eleven years, streaked and smeared from head to foot with ink, stopped me. His brown hair fell over his forehead, and he looked me up and down with a sharp gaze.

"What d'ye want, girl?" he asked rudely. I bristled.

"I am here to see Master Caxton," I informed him as haughtily as I could. "Is he within?"

The boy studied me for some moments and then motioned me toward the back room. In it, lines were strung from one wall to the other, and printed pages fluttered from them, drying. Master Caxton was bent over a table, studying a page black with ink.

"Come over here, Nell," he called, beckoning to me without looking up. I came to his side and looked at the page. The letters were thick and even, the lines of type straight and true.

"It's beautiful," I said. "What is it?"

"It is a page from Lord Rivers's *Dictes and Sayings of the Philosophers.*"

I was surprised. "The prince's uncle? The same Lord Rivers who is with him in Ludlow?"

"The same," Master Caxton replied. "A brilliant man, very well-read. It was he who set up this shop for me."

I mulled this over. I had always considered Lord Rivers a stiff and distant man. In the palace, he was mocked secretly for the rumor that he wore an itchy, painful hair shirt under his robes to prove his humility and religious devotion. But hearing that he was Master Caxton's patron, I thought perhaps he was not as bad as I had assumed. And he had written a book!

"Let me show you the shop before we begin," Master Caxton said. He rose and took me back into the front room, motioning to the wood-and-metal device.

"This is the printing press," Master Caxton told me. "Over here is the type—the letters, which we use to form the words. Here is the ink. Now, watch my compositor while he sets a page."

The compositor, a heavily muscled man, began to place the small blocks of type into a metal frame, letter by letter, while Master Caxton explained his actions to me.

"That is Master Wynkyn de Worde, child. There's none finer in our business. See, as he finishes each line of type he places it in the forme here. When the forme holds an entire page, he puts it into the press.

"Next, the forme must be inked. You can see that is a rather messy job. Jacob, my printer's devil, does that."

I watched as the brown-haired boy, Jacob, rolled black ink over the metal letters in the forme. Master de Worde pulled a lever, straining at the weight, and the muscles on his arms stood out. Metal groaned and moved, and the top of the press came down on the forme, pressing the paper tightly against the inked letters.

When Master de Worde lifted the press, we looked at the result: a page of bright black letters on clean white paper. A page of a book, all done on a machine! I was openmouthed with wonder.

"Close your mouth or a bird'll fly in," Jacob mocked. I glared at him.

"It *is* a wonder," Master Caxton said mildly. "We can print as many copies of that page as we have paper for, and so with the next page and the next. We could print enough books for all of Westminster to read Lord Rivers's work."

"Aye, if any of Westminster could read!" chortled Master de Worde, his accent thick, and Master Caxton laughed.

"Well, soon enough there'll be *one* native of Westminster who can read what the philosophers have to say!" The master clapped me on the back so hard I stumbled forward, catching myself on an ink-stained shelf. I pulled back black fingers.

"Now you're one of us, girl!" Master de Worde said, pointing to my dirty hands. He smiled at me, and I was suddenly very glad to be a part of this strange shop of inky letters, where words magically became sentences, sentences magically became pages, and pages magically became books.

I studied my letters with Master Caxton three times a week, and I helped in his shop beneath the sign of the Red Pale with the little chores I could do—sweeping the sawdust, filling the inkpots, carefully hanging the printed pages to dry. I loved every moment of it, and thrilled at how the letters I learned developed slowly into words, just as they did when Wynkyn de Worde placed them in the forme.

Jacob seemed to resent me at first. He didn't address me by name, but called me "your ladyship"—and not respectfully. He dropped paper scraps on a floor I'd just swept, or dribbled ink on a clean tabletop when my back was turned. I collected all the scraps, though, and kept them, using them to practice my letters, for paper was expensive and hard to come by.

And I got my revenge: one wintry afternoon, Jacob left his muddy boots at the door when he came in, and I filled them with pen nibs too worn to be used for writing. At the end of the day, when he pulled his boots back on, the sharp nibs jabbed his feet. He shouted, and Wynkyn de Worde, who'd watched me place the nibs, burst into guffaws as Jacob shook out the boots and watched the tips roll across the floor.

"Is this my punishment for smearing a page, Master de Worde?" Jacob demanded, but the compositor shook his head.

" 'Twasn't me, boy!" he protested, smiling. "Though if I'd thought of it . . ."

Jacob glared at me then, and my shoulders shook with suppressed laughter. "I must have dropped them by mistake," I said meekly.

For a moment I wasn't sure which way the situation would turn, but then Jacob, too, started to laugh.

"Well played, Lady Nell!" It was the first time he'd said my name. And even if he still mocked me, at least he showed then that he knew who I was.

After that, when Jacob had a break from his duties, he would sometimes help me compose simple sentences, or write out lines for me to practice reading. He wasn't the most patient of boys, and he would sigh or roll his eyes at my frequent mistakes. But I worked hard, both at my tasks and at my English studies, and because he was helping me he took pride in my advances, even offering an occasional word of praise. He was warming to me after all.

At last I was able to write a few lines, and I wrote my first letter to Ned. When I asked Jacob to help me with the spelling, he examined what I'd written:

From Eleanor Gould of Westminster to His Grace Prince Edward, Greetings:

I too can write, but not in Latin. When will you visit? Is Ludlow verry bad? I hope to meet again soon.

He looked up at me. "You're writing to the Prince of Wales?" he asked. His lips twitched.

"Indeed I am," I replied, my tone as confident as I could make it. "Is there anything wrong with that?"

"Well . . ." His voice trailed off as he tried to decide what exactly he should say. He knew nothing of my past. To him, I was merely a strange girl who, for no apparent reason, wished to write to a prince. But he must have liked something about the idea, for instead of teasing me or refusing to help, he finally grinned and said, "*Very* has only one *r*."

Papa took my letter to the palace, and he told me that one of the queen's attendants assured him it would be sent with the next packet going to Ludlow. For weeks, I was feverish with anticipation waiting for a reply. Each day I asked Papa if he had brought back a letter, and his answer was always no.

At last, however, Papa came home waving a parchment page. In the months I had been learning to read and write, Ned's own skills had improved greatly. He wrote, in English this time:

Ludlow is quite dull. I study very much. The food is bad, but Uncle Rivers is good to me. I am learning the sword and bow. I am so glad you can write to me.

Each letter I received was like a little visit from Ned. I kept these missives in a wooden case by my bed, reading and rereading them, and slowly the stack grew as I turned ten, and then eleven.

Then, one late winter day, I got a letter that sent me running through the house with joy and excitement.

His Grace my father the king must go to France. You may know there will be war. He wishes to knight me. I am to be the guardian of the realm while he is gone. I will be home sometime after Lady Day. Will your father bring you to see me?

Ned was coming home!

CHAPTER FIVE

It was more than two weeks before Ned and I finally met face-to-face again.

We hadn't seen each other for years, and at first we were awkward together. He greeted me formally, and I curtsied, as I supposed one should do to the guardian of the realm. When I looked up, though, I saw his eyes sparkling, and he began to laugh.

"Lady Nell!" he said.

"My lord," I replied, giggling.

At once the Ned of years before came back, and he took my hand and pulled me through the halls, past attendants and courtiers who, to my amazement, bowed deeply to him as we passed. He seemed unimpressed by this, but it made me realize, as I had never done before, that here was the boy who would one day be king. And he held my hand!

We talked for hours that day, sitting in a dusty, little-used room down the hall from the old nursery. There was no furniture in it at all, but there was one big window with a stone window seat, and we perched there while I described Master Caxton's shop and my studies, and he told me about Ludlow—the details that he dared not put in a letter for fear it might be read by others.

"Uncle Rivers is a good man, nearly a holy man," he said. "But oh, Nell! There are few things more tiresome than a holy man. Prayers and more prayers, and no music. And no laughter— I feel like this is the first time I've so much as smiled in a year!"

I could see that his uncle's solemnity had affected Ned. He was quieter, more reflective, and he thought a great deal about being a king and how he would govern.

"I love this kingdom," he told me. "I want to see more of it—I want to see it all. Not as a prince, but on my own, so I can meet the people who will be my subjects and find out what they need, what they *want* in their ruler. When I'm older I'll ride the length and breadth of England and speak to everyone I meet—monks, shoemakers, everyone."

"Are you still afraid to become king?" I asked him.

He mused on my question, his face reflecting the ideas that came and went.

"I'm afraid that I won't do it well," he admitted at last. "It's so much of a burden. The safety, the happiness, of a whole people! How can anyone bear that? And the endless wars with France—you know I will have to go to war if I am king."

"You could make peace," I suggested, and he smiled.

"We were at war with France for nearly a hundred years," he said. "And now we are again. I don't think it will ever stop.

The French want our throne; we want theirs. Back and forth it goes, and will always go."

The idea made him sound weary, so I changed the subject. "What *is* a guardian of the realm? Will you rule?"

"No! Not really. It's just a title, truthfully. The king's council will govern, and Uncle Richard will oversee the kingdom."

I made a face. I still remembered Richard of Gloucester's stony eyes and cheerless presence—and how he tried to have me humiliated.

Ned laughed. "Uncle Richard's not so bad. He's very learned, you know—he even founded a college. And he's a fine soldier. He's kept peace in the north for years. Even Father thought that wasn't possible."

"I've never seen him smile," I noted.

Ned thought for a minute, then nodded. "He's not a cheerful person. His back pains him often, and I think that makes him sour. But he never complains, and no one was ever more loyal to my father than he was, through all those years of war—with Henry, with the Scots, with the French, with everyone."

"I don't care," I said. "I don't like him."

"Luckily, I do," Ned said. "He's lord chamberlain now, and the most powerful man in the kingdom after Father. I'll have to see him constantly."

"Poor you!" I mocked him, and he laughed again. But his eyes were grave, and I got some small sense of the weight that he would carry. There was little I could do but listen and ask questions, secretly thrilling to the warmth of his fingers twined with mine.

· • ·

I left the palace alone that evening, for Papa still had work to do in the kitchens. On my way out, I passed through the Great Hall, invisible as always amid the flow of courtiers and servants and guards. As I hurried, head down, my heel caught on the loose hem of my dress and I stumbled.

A hand on my arm righted me. "Girl," a low voice said, and I looked up, startled.

Richard of Gloucester stood beside me. He seemed to have appeared out of nowhere, as if Ned and I had conjured him by talking about him.

"My lord," I said, gulping. I couldn't curtsy; his grip on my arm was too tight.

"You are the child with the ball," he said. It was not a question. He meant that night Ned and I had tossed our ball over the railing and overturned a lady's wine cup. The night he had wanted me punished. That had been years ago—how odd that he remembered it.

"Yes, my lord."

"What is your name?"

"Nell Gould, my lord."

"Nell Gould," he repeated. I didn't like the sound of my name on his lips. "And how fares my nephew, our realm's new guardian?" His gaze was like a candle flame, flickering and hot.

I had the strange thought that I was in danger of being burned, but I didn't dare pull away.

"He . . . he is well, my lord," I replied.

"I am glad to hear it. He does not really speak to me, only to his uncle Rivers. So you see I am reduced to asking after his health from his playmates!" The duke smiled, but there was no humor in it.

"He is very close to Lord Rivers," I said.

"Indeed. Tell me. Does young Ned feel that his role as guardian is too great a responsibility?"

I blinked and wondered what to answer. What exactly did he want to know?

But then I realized that I didn't want to tell this man anything, anything at all. "He doesn't speak to me of such matters, my lord," I lied, as humbly as I could. "I try to take his mind off all that."

"Indeed," the duke said again. "I am sure you do!"

With that he released me, and I scurried away, my heart beating hard. When I looked back I saw him gazing after me, his expression hard and thoughtful.

That night I stood before the looking glass and pulled up the sleeve of my nightdress. On my arm were the marks of Richard of Gloucester's fingers, as clear as if they were painted on my skin. I shuddered and tugged my sleeve down, and I never spoke of the encounter to Papa or to Ned.

· • ·

Ned sent for me a few times before King Edward left for France, and we were able to be together as we once had been, whirling through the palace halls and grounds in childish games that, for a short while, erased all worry from Ned's eyes. We admired the new baby, Princess Anne, and I spent time with Cecily, who was as high-spirited and good-humored as ever. I even brought Toby with me, and he played happily with Prince Dickon, who was but a few days younger than he. They quickly became friends, and I was pleased to see it.

But after the king left for France in the spring, Ned had to attend meeting after meeting in his new role as guardian. In our brief hours together, he described the endless droning of councilors, the bewildering assortment of foreign ambassadors and dignitaries whom he was expected to remember and greet by name each time they met. I tried to entertain him with stories: the palace cook who'd sliced off the tip of his finger and then couldn't find it, so a whole dinner had to be thrown away and started over. The fight between the tanner and the cobbler over the tanner's horse, which every morning left a steaming pile in front of the cobbler's shop. The day the pigs escaped from the Monastery of St. Anthony and rampaged through the streets, knocking down merchants and lords alike. I was always glad when I could make him laugh.

I went less often to Master Caxton's shop. He was understanding; I suppose Father had explained my friendship with Ned. But Jacob needled me about it.

"Are you too important to work with us now, Lady Nell?" he asked when I stopped in to check on a translation of the Latin writer Cicero. I had helped with the printing from the very first page, and I was proud of it.

I made a face at him. "I was always too important to work with you," I retorted. I returned to looking at the day's pages, pleased with the dark, straight lines of type.

"Such an eminent girl should know the Latin this was written in," Jacob said.

I rolled my eyes. "It's in English now."

"So you don't want to learn Latin?"

I wasn't sure I understood. "Are you—are you offering to teach me?"

He smiled, saying nothing.

"Oh Jacob, would you? I do want to learn! Really—I'll do anything!"

"Oh, I know you will," he said. "You'll clean the formes, is what you'll do." It was the dirtiest job in the shop, but I would do it gladly in exchange. At last, I would learn Latin!

King Edward's invasion of France lasted only two months. It seemed that neither he nor France's King Louis really wanted to fight again, after long, exhausting years of conflict. To make peace, King Louis agreed to give King Edward a great deal of money, and King Edward agreed that Princess Bess would marry the crown prince of France, the dauphin. She would, on King Louis's death, become queen of France.

I marveled to think of the little girl I had played with sitting on the throne of a country so great and distant as France. I didn't envy her, though, for the dauphin was said to be both ugly and sickly and she had never met him. But Bess was thrilled.

"I shall be queen of France!" she crowed as she primped at the mirror in her new rooms. The reflection that gazed back at her was the very image of her mother, blond and beautiful, her brow high and her skin like the smoothest silk satin.

She was no longer housed with the other princes and princesses, but had stately rooms of her own, as befitted a young betrothed woman. She practiced being queen with Cecily, Mary, and me—we took turns curtsying and obeying her orders, and she insisted we call her Madame la Dauphine instead of Bess.

Not everyone was as excited as she at the news of this settlement, though. I was passing through the private hallways of the palace some days later when I heard two men talking—and I realized one was Richard of Gloucester. I had no desire to see him again; the bruises he left on me last time had taken weeks to fade. So I ducked behind a stone column, breathing as quietly as I could.

"It's perfidy—a *disgrace*, this French treaty!" I heard Richard snap.

"That is strong language, brother," the other man cautioned. It was Ned's younger uncle, George, the Duke of Clarence.

Richard snorted. "Our brother has been humiliated, don't you see? He is too enthralled by wine and women to pay proper attention to the needs of the kingdom. *No battle*—and I'd sent a thousand archers to fight!"

"Richard—"

"He's been paid off by France like a lowly servant—even traded away his daughter! There's no honor in it, none!"

"But Richard—"

"We will go and see the king of France ourselves."

"Oh, I'm not sure that would be a good idea," Clarence said nervously. "Edward wouldn't be pleased at all."

"Do you think I care one whit if Edward is pleased? He's as much as betrayed his country with this treaty!" Richard snarled.

I held my breath. That statement was treading very close to treason. If they saw me now . . .

But the two men, still arguing, stormed off in the direction they'd come from, and I stepped out from my hiding place shaking. I told no one what I'd heard. To speak openly of treason—even if it was someone else's—was only asking for trouble. Especially if that someone was the king's brother.

Such matters were above me, but I trembled the whole way home, and did not sleep easily.

Only a few weeks later, though, news came that the king of France had gifted Richard some fine horses and a set of gold-plated tableware, and that Richard had gone with King Edward to Paris to accept the treaty formally. It hadn't taken much to change his mind—but I wasn't surprised. I didn't think of him as a man of principle, no matter what he said to the Duke of Clarence about *honor* and *perfidy*. There was too much slyness in him.

In September, King Edward returned from France. From

just outside the shop, Papa, Toby, and I watched his triumphal procession down King Street, though I could barely see a thing in the great crowd of people. Toby sat on Papa's shoulders and called out the sights from his vantage point above the throng.

"There are a hundred men with trumpets, at least!" he reported. This we could tell by hearing. "And the guildmasters have come out to greet the king. They wear all different colored robes. They are very fine! Ah—here he is! It's the king! Papa, he is so big!"

Indeed, King Edward had grown stout; we'd heard that his gilded armor had to be remade before he left for France, and again while he was there. Rumor had it that his breath was short and his energy limited. Still, he cut a grand figure as he rode past us, the sun shining on his golden hair, his fur-trimmed velvet cape fluttering behind him, his smile flashing as the crowd roared. He delighted in his subjects' love, laughing his great laugh and waving as the cheers rose around him.

Ned went back to Ludlow after a week of celebration. I didn't see him at all during that week, and I felt his absence very keenly after spending so much time together.

To distract myself I studied hard with Master Caxton, and worked longer hours at the shop beneath the sign of the Red Pale. Jacob tutored me in Latin whenever Master Caxton was away, and I picked it up quickly. He had become a good and patient teacher, full of compliments when I conjugated a verb correctly, quick with a joke when I misused a word. It wasn't long before I could make out whole sentences in the untranslated works of

Cicero. And when I wrote my first letter to Ned in Latin, his shocked, pleased reply made me even gladder that I'd spent the time and effort to learn.

After Ned left, I went to the palace less often, though I visited Cecily sometimes when Toby went to play with Prince Dickon under Nurse's watchful eye. One winter evening we sat sipping cider before a crackling fire in the nursery, and Cecily said, in a low voice, "Nell, I am betrothed."

I thought I had misheard her. But one look at her downcast face told me otherwise.

"I hadn't heard," I said carefully.

"It hasn't been announced yet." She was quiet for a moment, then burst out, "I hope it never is!"

"Who is your intended?"

"King James of Scotland's son. He's James also."

"Is there . . . something wrong with him?"

"No," Cecily admitted. "He's said to be handsome, and not entirely stupid."

"Then why don't you want to be betrothed to him?"

"Scotland!" she fumed. "Have you been to Scotland?" Of course I had not, but she didn't really want an answer. "It's the coldest, rainiest, bleakest place there is. All mists and mud and sheep. I don't want to leave England. I don't want to leave my family to marry a man I don't know!"

There was nothing I could say that would help. I put a hand on hers, but she shrugged it off. In one quick movement she stood, picked up her ceramic cider cup, and threw it as hard as she could into the fire. The cup shattered, and the cider flared up in the flame.

"Cecily . . ." I began, startled.

"I know." She sat again, breathing heavily. "We're pawns, all we daughters. One is for France, one for Scotland. And what treaty or territory will Mary guarantee, and Anne?" Her tone was bitter.

"I'll visit you in Scotland," I said, feeling helpless.

She gazed into the fire another moment more, then smiled at me, pushing down her anger. "I should like that. But be sure to bring your warmest cloak."

Toby and Dickon came in then, and we talked tactfully of other things until she went off to bed. Toby curled up by the fire, drowsing with Dickon as we waited for Papa to fetch us. I had nearly dozed off myself when I heard angry voices in the hall. Alarmed, I tiptoed to the door and listened intently.

"How dare you?" a woman hissed. "It is bad enough that I have to see that harlot downstairs day after day. How dare you bring her to our chambers—past your own children's rooms?"

The door was open a crack, and I peered through. In the dim torchlit hallway, I could make out two figures. One was the woman who had spoken, the other a man, tall and wide and golden-haired.

I caught my breath.

"Calm yourself, Elizabeth," King Edward said, low. "Do you want your ladies to hear the queen of England shouting like a fishwife?"

"I do not care who hears me," the queen replied in a tremulous voice. "You shame me, husband, and you shame yourself."

The king inhaled sharply. When he spoke, his voice shook too, but with anger. "Have you forgotten who I am, milady? Do you dare to reprimand me?"

There was no answer. I heard the clattering of the queen's shoes on the stone floor, and the louder, angrier thud of the king's boots as they stormed away in opposite directions. When all was quiet I peered through the door again—and then clasped a hand to my mouth to stifle my gasp of shock.

A man lurked, motionless and silent, in the shadows. He was so well hidden that I almost did not notice him, but even in the darkness, the slim, stiff bearing and grim face told me clearly that it was Richard of Gloucester. He had watched the whole quarrel unseen—just as I had.

He stepped out into the light of the wall torch, and I was too slow to avoid his seeing me. His raised eyebrow showed clearly that he knew exactly who I was, and that he had heard what I heard. For an instant we stared at each other, unspeaking. Then I bobbed a curtsy, eased back into the nursery, and ran to my seat by the fire. There was no sound but the crackle of flame, but my heart raced.

It was only a few days later that I began to understand what the royal argument had been about. Toby and I had spent the afternoon in the nursery, and when Papa came for us a woman passed us in the hall. I'd never noticed her before; she was a plump beauty with flaxen curls whose eyes flashed at my father as she walked by.

"Who is that?" I asked Papa.

"No one you need concern yourself with," he said shortly, pulling me along.

Of course, this only whetted my curiosity, so I asked Princess Cecily about her the next time I came to the palace to fetch Toby.

"That is Jane Shore, our father's mistress," she replied, looking around to make sure no one overheard. As she stitched green thread through an embroidered pillow cover I nodded wisely, unsure of what she meant. We talked of Ned and the other princesses for the rest of my visit, for I didn't feel comfortable asking her more about it.

That night, as we sat before the fire, I asked Papa.

"Who is Jane Shore?"

He gave me a searching look. "You're old enough to understand," he said at last, and I laid aside my stitching. "She is mistress to the king. Do you know what that means?"

I shook my head.

"She is the king's woman." I thought about the way Jane Shore had looked at my father, and then about what I'd heard between the king and queen. All at once I realized what he was talking about. My cheeks grew warm.

"But . . . what of the queen?"

"She knows. He is the king. He may do as he pleases." In Papa's voice was the only censure of King Edward I ever heard from him. I didn't ask anything more, but at the press the next day, Jacob told me that there were other women, many others, and there had been for years.

"Children, too," he said, rolling the ink over the forme to print a page. "Four bastards . . . maybe more." I looked down at my feet, embarrassed that I hadn't known—I, who had been raised among King Edward's own family. The palace, I was learning, was full of secrets.

· ● ·

One dreary December afternoon, Toby came home from a day at court bursting with news and excitement. "*Nell! Nell!*" he shouted, running into the hall, his cloak wet with winter rain and his boots muddied.

"Toby, your boots!" I scolded. "Take them off before you speak another word." He wriggled and twitched as I helped him with his outdoor clothes. "Now, what is your news?"

"Dickon is getting married!" he announced.

"Married! But he's only five!" Surprised, I looked at Papa over Toby's wet head. Royalty and nobles were often betrothed young, but the actual marriages usually took place much later.

Papa nodded. "He's to marry the Duchess of Norfolk. She's all of six years old herself. Very wealthy, of course, with vast tracts of land. A marriage gives the king access to those lands, and the money that goes with them."

"Ah," I said. Royal marriages were always alliances for money or land.

Toby was hopping about with excitement. "Dickon says that

I can go to the wedding! Can I, Papa? Will you go too? Papa, I want to be married. Can I get married too?"

Papa caught Toby in a bear hug, asking with a smile, "And who would you marry, my boy?"

"Oh, I think Princess Cecily," Toby said confidently. Papa and I hooted with laughter at the idea, but Toby glared at us. "I *shall* marry her!" he insisted.

"She's to marry the prince of Scotland," I reminded him, for the announcement had been formally made a few weeks earlier. Toby scowled.

"As for the wedding, Toby," Papa said, "if we receive an invitation, then surely we can go. But if not, we will watch the festivities from the street as our neighbors do."

I never expected that we would attend, so when a messenger arrived bearing our invitation, lettered beautifully on creamy parchment, I was stunned. Prince Dickon must have thrown quite a tantrum to get a butcher's family invited to his wedding!

We ordered fine new clothes for the occasion. I had my first grown-up gown, high-waisted in blue silk with an embroidered belt, and I wore a tall, pointed steeple hat with a short gauze veil. When I turned this way and that before the looking glass, I barely recognized myself.

Papa and Toby, too, were grand in red houppelande robes and round hats. Mathilda admired us from all angles as we made ready to go to St. Stephen's Chapel, where the wedding Mass was to take place.

We stood far in the back. Toby and I could see little, but

what we did see was very impressive indeed. The parade of nobility, the entrance of the royal family, the finest velvets and silks, the long wedding Mass, the singing of the choir—how beautiful it all was! Toby was transfixed as he strained to hear his friend vow to love and honor his tiny wife forever. The little duchess wobbled beneath the weight of her robes, and I feared she might collapse from the effort of standing so long, but she did well, her pointy pale face weary and confused as she turned to face the cheering crowd when the ceremony ended.

As the royal party passed out of the chapel, I was astonished to see Ned, his blond curls and bright blue eyes unmistakable. I had not heard that he would be back from Ludlow for his brother's wedding! I tried to catch his eye, but in the crush of people it was impossible.

Then, as we were exiting St. Stephen's, a messenger came up to me. "Mistress Gould?" he asked. I nodded, and he pressed a note into my palm. Quickly I read it:

Come to the palace. The usual place.

It was unsigned, but the hand was Ned's.

As Papa was going to the kitchens to oversee the handling of the meats for the wedding banquet, it was no difficulty for me to go along with him. I left him in the supply cellars and walked up the stone stairs and through the long halls to the gallery over the banquet hall, where I could see servants rushing about below as they prepared the room for feasting, music, and mummery.

I had not been waiting long before Ned joined me. I hugged him tightly, feeling new height and new muscle from his training at arms. We were eleven now, and he had changed.

"Oh Nell, I have missed you!" Ned exclaimed, releasing me. "Why, you are quite grown up!" Under his appraising look, I was glad I still wore my wedding finery, though I'd replaced my tall hat with a simple cap.

"Were you surprised to be invited to the wedding?" he asked me.

"Utterly!" I said. "I could hardly believe the queen would allow it. I imagine Dickon must have made a terrible fuss."

"It was his idea, but I executed it—without a fuss."

"Well, it was lovely, and I thank you for it."

We stood at the gallery railing, looking at the scene below. "Do you know," Ned said, "there are no girls or women at Ludlow? Every day I see nothing but beards. Even the cows are horned in Wales, and I believe the chickens crow like roosters."

I laughed, relieved that he had not wholly changed. He was still sweet and funny, still watched life with a measured eye.

"It sounds deadly dull," I told him. "What fun is there without women? There's no dancing, nor good conversation. Nothing but sport and combat, combat and sport."

"It's true," Ned said with a groan. "I rise at six, go to Mass, study, eat, practice horsemanship and swordplay, go to Vespers, eat, study, and sleep. I shall be the most dreary king that ever ruled. But that's Father's intention—that I should have all his skills and none of his faults."

I remembered what Bess had said about their father, years before: *He doesn't want Ned to be like him. He wants him to be better. Smarter.* I understood now.

Ned sighed, then changed the subject. "And what about you, Nell? Now that you know Latin, do you plan to go to university to be a scholar? Will you become a clerk?"

He was teasing, but I was surprised—and a little hurt—nevertheless. Ned knew neither of those was a possibility. I was a girl.

"I will get married, no doubt," I said sharply. "Maybe to Nick, the chandler's son, or Adam the cooper. He's a widower and only twenty years older than I am. I'll have half a dozen children and run a household. Probably I'll forget my Latin by the time I'm thirty."

He looked abashed. "That was stupid of me, Nell. I'm sorry."

"I suppose it was a waste of time to learn it. Even your sisters have no real use for their Latin," I pointed out. "Except to read the Bible, if the priest allows it. Oh, maybe I'll become a nun!"

"Stop!" Ned protested. "You—a nun? I can't even imagine it." I had to smile at the idea myself. "But you can read, Nell, and write. In two languages. Perhaps you could be my personal clerk, when I'm king. Wouldn't that be grand?"

It was a fantastical thought, almost an absurdity, but I loved it.

"I could do it."

"I know you could."

"We would be together often. Your queen might be jealous.

If you even have one, I mean. How will you ever win a queen? Stuck with the boys and men at Ludlow, you'll have no talent at wooing. No royal princess will ever want you."

A gleam came to Ned's eye. "Then I shall have to practice!" he declared, and lunged for me. I dodged away from him, and he chased me up and down the gallery. Finally, beneath a portrait of Edward the Third, bearded and solemn, he caught me.

"So you think I'll never win a queen, do you?" he challenged. "I've won you, haven't I?"

Suddenly the game was no longer fun for me. Ned *would* have a queen someday, and it would not be me. Another girl, a royal princess from some foreign place, would be his confidante, his dearest friend. I hated the thought of it.

Ned saw how my face changed, and he let me go. He looked at me with sudden awareness, almost as if he could tell what I was thinking, and I felt myself flush. Then he pulled a ring off his finger.

"Nell, will you take this?" He held it out to me. It was a hammered gold band with his initials, *E P*, *Edward Princeps*, on it.

"What . . . ?" I whispered. Such a token could not mean anything, between us. I knew that. Yet why would he give it?

"I can't—I cannot promise myself to you," Ned said. "I must marry royalty, or at least nobility, like Dickon did. You know that, don't you?" His eyes searched my face, and I nodded. "But you might have need of me sometime. If you show this, you will be able to get to me."

I was puzzled, and heartsore. I couldn't bear to think of

him marrying another, and I couldn't imagine what he meant when he said I might have need of him. Still, I pulled off my own ring, a shimmering white moonstone set in silver that Papa had given me for my last name day.

"Then you take this," I said. "And if ever you need *me*, send it. I will come to you."

Ned smiled and took the ring, placing it on his little finger. His I later had to string on a chain around my neck, for already his fingers were much larger than mine.

"You should get back to the festivities," I said at last. I didn't want him to go.

"Yes, I must. Watch the banquet from here, Nell," he told me. "I'll see you again soon." He squeezed my hand and was gone, leaving me to trace his initials on the gold band that meant nothing—nothing except, to me, all the world.

CHAPTER SIX

"Nell, have you heard? The duke is dead!"

Mistress Makepiece, the cobbler's wife, called this across the street to me as I swept dirty snow from the front of the shop. A month before, Mathilda had married Tom, the draper's journeyman, and gone to live with him, and now I did many of her chores, though we had hired a cook and a maidservant to take up some slack.

"What?" I said, laying aside my broom. "Which duke? What's happened?"

Mistress Makepiece picked her way across the street, avoiding the piles of horse dung that the cleaners had not yet removed.

"The king's brother—the Duke of Clarence. He's dead!"

Ned's uncle George had recently been arrested and imprisoned in the Tower. It was said that he had plotted against the king, which was treason. I recalled eavesdropping on him and Richard after the king's invasion of France, and how foolish and easily swayed he had seemed. I knew he had sided with the king's enemies once, before I was born. His father-in-law, the Earl of Warwick, had been an ally of King Henry the Sixth during the Wars of the Roses, and George had conspired with him. Before long, though, George grew disenchanted with the earl and declared his support for King Edward again, and the king forgave him. I wondered if he would dare be so disloyal a second time. Still, like everyone who lived outside the palace walls, I was often befuddled by what happened within them.

"How did he die?" I asked. "Was he ill?"

"He drowned," Mistress Makepiece said, her eyes wide.

"Drowned? In the Tower? Did he fall into the Thames?" The river ran just beside the complex of buildings that made up the Tower.

"No." Mistress Makepiece lowered her voice. "He was drowned in a butt of Malmsey wine."

"What?" I stared at her. "That's ridiculous. How can anyone drown in a barrel of wine?"

"They say the other brother did it," she whispered. "Richard of Gloucester."

I shivered. I recalled Papa, years before, saying that people had blamed Richard for the death of poor King Henry. Still, no man could kill his own brother . . . could he?

"You shouldn't repeat such a story," I said sharply. "I'm sure it's false—or worse, treasonous!"

Mistress Makepiece narrowed her eyes at me and snorted. Then she turned on her heel and trotted back across to her own shop, where the iron sign of a man holding a shoe swung in the cold wind.

When Papa came home I asked him about the rumors.

"The Duke of Gloucester is not in town and hasn't been since Dickon's wedding," he replied sternly. "He's in the north, where he rules fairly and well. You shouldn't listen to Mary Makepiece's gossip. People make up many stories about the duke, and there's little truth in any of it."

He said no more, and I tried to forget the story, but in truth it was easy to believe it. Richard of Gloucester's grimness and anger, in the midst of a court full of light and liveliness, had always frightened me. Even at a banquet, sitting with his wife, the Lady Anne, he never smiled, and to me the music always sounded more somber when he was in the room.

· ● ·

King Edward changed after the Duke of Clarence's death. He was rarely in Westminster anymore, and when he was, he spent little time at the palace. Instead, he wandered the streets almost unattended, stopping at taverns to eat and drink with lords who were his friends—and ladies who were more than his friends. This undignified behavior made tongues wag. People began to resent him for his excesses, but he seemed not to care.

On a late winter afternoon, I was in Master Caxton's shop helping Jacob ink a page on the press when a commotion sounded in the street outside. Suddenly the shop door flew open.

There stood King Edward, huge, golden, robed in furs against the bitter wind.

His few attendants followed him into the main room, and I knelt quickly; Jacob, now an apprentice, did the same. Master Caxton emerged from his office. It was the only time I ever saw him at a loss for words. He bowed, and opened his mouth, but nothing came out.

Finally King Edward spoke. "Master Caxton, I have it on the authority of Lord Rivers and de Gruthuyese of Bruges that you are the best printer in England."

Master Caxton gulped. "Your Majesty is too kind," he murmured, and bowed again.

"Nonsense!" King Edward said. "I've seen your work myself. I have many of your books. Fine printing, fine! And what is on the press today?"

"Ah! Your Majesty, this is a remarkable work, a most unusual book. *The Canterbury Tales*, by one Geoffrey Chaucer," said Master Caxton, in his element now. "Perhaps you know it? He wrote it just a hundred years ago, while your great-great-grandfather King Edward the Third reigned. May I present a copy to Your Majesty?" He backed over to the bookshelf that held our finished work, pulled out a bound book, and handed it to the king.

"By the saints," King Edward swore, "this is a heavy book!" He thumbed through it. "Yes, I know this! 'When April with his showers hath pierced the drought / Of March with sweetness to the very root . . .' Those lines have always made me long for spring when the winter winds blow cold as they do today. I shall enjoy rereading it, I am sure."

As the king turned to leave, his eye fell on me and he frowned. "Stand up, girl," he demanded. I rose, trembling. I was almost too frightened to speak. Though I had been in the palace a hundred times, played with the princes and princesses, and spoken with the queen, the king's presence was still overwhelming. I had not been so close to him since the day I had bounced that ball onto his banquet table, years before.

"You look familiar," the king mused. "Who are you?"

"M-My father is John Gould, the butcher, Your Majesty," I stammered. "I was born—"

"On the same day as the Prince of Wales!" the king finished for me. "Now I know you. You and my son are friends, are you not?"

It seemed presumptuous of me to claim to be a friend of the prince's, so I hedged: "We have played together, Your Majesty. And we—we write to each other. To practice our grammar."

The king took my chin in his huge hand and tilted my face upward. He studied me for a long moment, and then he smiled. His skin was very flushed, and broken blood vessels lined his nose and cheeks. He didn't look well. Still, in his smile I could see the King Edward of years past, before drink and excess had thickened and coarsened his handsome features. And in his eyes—though they were red-rimmed and hooded with flesh—I could see the same intelligence that I saw in Ned's.

"Be a friend to him, then, child," the king told me. "Ned will need his friends, I've no doubt."

"Yes, Your Majesty," I whispered, and sank in a low curtsy.

The next minute the king was gone, sweeping from the room in a rush of cold air, and we were left blinking in disbelief.

"Well," Master Caxton said at last. "Back to work. That was Lord Ratcliffe's copy of the *Tales*, and he expects it today. We have three hundred seventy-four pages to print!"

The door opened again, startling us, and one of the king's attendants hurried in. He handed a purse to Master Caxton, said, "With His Majesty's compliments," and exited as swiftly as he'd come.

Master Caxton opened the purse, and we gasped as he poured its coins onto an oak table. Twenty gold nobles in all— as much as the shop might make in six months!

We danced around the press gleefully, and when Jacob grasped me about the waist and did a country step with me, I spun and laughed until my hair spilled out of my cap, and the shop whirled even after I had stopped.

· ● ·

We were able to print more books after the king's generous bonus, and one afternoon Jacob took me aside to show me a new volume he was setting up in the forme.

"Look at this," he said, pointing to a just-printed title page.

My hands were clean, so I picked it up. It read: *The Boke of St. Albans.*

"What is it?" I asked. He motioned me to read the letters in the forme. They were laid backwards, like a mirror image, but by then I had grown accustomed to reading them that way.

It was a table of contents, the list of the book's chapter titles.

I read the chapters aloud: "The maner to speake of Hawkes from an egge till they be able to be taken. How you shall take Hawkes, with what instruments, and how you shall kidde them. When your Hawke may be drawne to reclaime, and the manner of her diet. How to feede your hawke and know her infirmities. When your Hawke shall bathe."

Again I asked, "What *is* this?"

"It's a treatise on hawking and hunting and fishing," Jacob replied.

"Yes, I figured that out," I said. "Do people really bathe hawks? With those talons?"

"It's by a writer named Juliana Berners."

I stared at him. "Juliana? The writer is a woman?"

"So it appears. I'm not sure I believe it. It could be a false name. Perhaps the author wanted to shock people—that might sell more copies."

I ran my hand over the page. "No," I said. "I'm sure it is by a woman." I wasn't certain if I was saying that to annoy him, or if I really believed it. But it would be wonderful if it were true.

"How could a woman write a book?" Jacob asked, in the tone he used to provoke me.

I looked at him sidelong. "What a question! She would put quill to paper, I suppose, like anyone else. Of course, she would need to know how to read and write. But I imagine anyone who had the learning could do it—or at least try it."

"Maybe so." Jacob grinned, his teeth flashing white in his inky face. "Maybe *you* should try it."

"I could never write a book," I protested. "What would I write about?"

"Oh, I don't know. Hunting, hawking? Fishing? Princes and princesses?" He was mocking me, but kindly. I met his brown eyes and saw something there I hadn't seen before. I wasn't sure what it was, but it both pleased and embarrassed me. I looked down quickly, back at the page.

"May I do this printing?" I asked. I had little interest in hawking and fishing, but I wanted to print a book written by a woman. Who knew when I would have another chance?

"Of course, if Master Caxton approves," Jacob said. "But you'll still have to clean the formes!"

It was thrilling to be in charge of *The Boke of St. Albans*. I was fascinated by every word, and learned far more about hawks, hunting, and fishing than I had ever wanted to know. The writer's detail was astonishing. She described taking hairs from a horse's tail to use as fishing lines, and dyeing them different colors to attract different fish at different times of the year. I imagined Dame Juliana as a noble lady with a great forested estate, someone who loved the sporting life so much she had to write about it, but Wynkyn de Worde told me she was a nun from St. Albans.

"A nun!" I said. "Why would a nun write about these things?"

He shrugged. "She was probably a noblewoman before she went into the convent. She'd have known all about hunting and fishing. Maybe she missed that life and wanted to live it again through her writing."

I mulled this over. Could writing do that for a person?

The more I worked on Dame Juliana's book, the more I found myself wondering about writing. Gradually, I thought about trying to write myself. But there was so little time, between caring for Toby and Papa and working at the press—and I had no idea why I wanted to or what I would say if I did.

When the printing was finally finished, I stood proudly as Master Caxton presented me with a leather-bound copy of the *Boke*. It was beautiful, the first book we had printed with colored illustrations—and the first book I had ever owned myself.

Before I left the press that day, Jacob took me aside. "I made something for you," he said, and pulled a little package from the vast pocket of his printer's apron.

I unwrapped it to find a small book, bound in red-brown leather, its spine sewn together with broad stitches. I thumbed through its pages, but they were blank. I looked at him, confused.

"It's for you to write in, if you choose to. I took the scraps from our printings, cut them to size, and bound them."

I turned the little book over and over, marveling at it. "It's wonderful," I said.

"It will be your very own book, written by Eleanor Gould—no false name!"

I made a face at him. "Nor is Juliana Berners a false name! But thank you, Jacob. This is a lovely gift. I'll use it—I promise."

And I did. The little notebook was easy to carry, and I

quickly fell into the habit of jotting down descriptions of events and thoughts as they happened.

A wagon full of ale barrels overturned in King Street this morning. Oh, the mad scramble as people tried to lift them and steal them away! One broke open, soaking the chandler's apprentice from head to foot. The stink of the beer and his dripping clothes made it very hard for him to deny his attempted theft!

· • ·

Does Jacob truly think I can write a book myself? If I could . . . perhaps a story like Chaucer's, a tale of a pilgrimage? But I have never been on pilgrimage. What do people who have never been anywhere or done anything write about?

I found I liked the feel of a quill scratching on paper, and I liked reading over what I had written. I called the notebook my book of secrets, because I wrote things in it that I wanted no one else to read.

· • ·

In May of that year, Princess Mary died.

She had contracted a wasting disease, and in desperation her mother brought her down the river to the royal palace at Greenwich, for the air was said to be better there. But it was to no avail; she died quickly.

I was terribly saddened, and I knew that the family was

devastated, for sweet, pretty Mary had been a favorite of everyone, and she was only fifteen. Ned came back for the funeral, but I didn't see him. I only heard of his sorrow through his letters, which made me weep to read.

It is too cruel that Mary is dead. Her face was so pale on her bier. She did not look like herself at all. She was always the best of us. She was not proud, like Bess, nor broody, like me, nor naughty, like Cecily. She was just kind and funny and good. I hope she is happy with God, but I feel I shall never be happy again.

I went with Toby to the palace to see Cecily after reading this. The halls were empty and echoing; the whole building seemed to be mourning the loss of the princess.

At last I found Cecily in the bedchamber she had shared with her sister. The cushioned chairs before the fireplace were empty of attendants, and the fireplace itself was cold. Cecily sat despondent on the high curtained bed she'd always shared with Mary, her face drawn with sorrow. Her black cap and veil made a sharp contrast against her white-blond hair.

"This will be my room alone now, Nell," she said to me, her blue eyes spilling tears. "I'll miss her so much!" The two of them had always been very close.

"I'm so sorry," I said, sitting beside her; she took my hands with hers, holding tight. "It isn't fair."

"She won't be at my wedding, Nell. How can that be?"

I blinked. "Your wedding? To James of Scotland?"

"Have you not heard? I am betrothed anew—to the duke of Albany. Alexander."

I hadn't heard. It must have happened recently, for the news had not yet spread. "But—what of Prince James? What of that betrothal?"

"His father and mine argued. There's been fighting along the border, you know, and Father wanted payment for the damage the Scots did. But King James refused."

"Who is Alexander, then? Is he handsome? Kind?" Cecily needed a kind man, now more than ever.

She shrugged. "He's the brother of the Scottish king. He hates his brother King James, so that pleases Father. Wealthy, I am sure—kind, I don't know. He's rather old—thirty, I think. But I have seen a portrait of him, and he seems . . . well, not unpleasant to look at. Not as handsome as Prince James, but tall, and strong—if you can believe the portrait."

I shook my head. Betrothed first to James, then to his uncle—it was true what Cecily had said, that the princesses were just pawns in the affairs of state. But she was too dejected to protest her fate today. And of course it would have done no good on any day.

"Is the wedding date set?"

"Not yet," Cecily said. "I will have time to get used to the idea—and used to the idea of Mary not being there. It's God's will, I suppose. But now that Ned is gone, and Bess as good as married, I feel so lonely. I wish you would visit more." She began to cry again, and I hugged her.

"I'll try," I said. She sounded so forlorn that I would have promised her almost anything.

"Do you remember—" I began. "Do you recall what happened with Mary and the poor fish?"

Cecily wiped her eyes. "The fish . . . oh, the fish! Those terrible fish with the sharp teeth, the ones in the pond. I do remember! Mary felt so badly for them that she tried to rescue one that was meant for the table—"

"She reached right into the water and grabbed it—"

"And it was so heavy it dragged her halfway in—"

"And Ned had to grab her feet and pull her back through the weeds and mud!"

Cecily gave a weepy snort of laughter. "We were in so much trouble! Lady Mistress Darcy threatened to tell Father, and Mary cried and cried until she forgave us."

"That was the only time I ever saw Mary get into trouble," I said.

"And she did it out of kindness. Kindness to a fish, but kindness nonetheless. It was so like her." Cecily's eyes welled up again.

I went back to Westminster Palace as often as I could in the next few months, and I wrote to Cecily during that time, nearly as often as I wrote to Ned. I told her how Toby was and tried to amuse her with gossip from King Street.

Master Simson the baker and Master Niles the other baker have decided to have a feud. Master Simson had a new sign made for his shop, very bright and large. Two days later, Master Niles had a new sign as well, even brighter and larger. Then Master Simson began to make cakes, which were Master Niles's specialty. Master Niles made his own cakes taller, so Master Simson made his higher still. The cakes grew and grew until each morning a crowd would gather outside the shops to see which baker had the tallest cake. Today, Master Niles came out with the tallest cake imaginable—nearly as high as Toby! And as he stepped back into his shop, the entire thing trembled, and wobbled, and then collapsed to the floor. Every child in King Street scrambled into the shop to get a free handful of cake!

Cecily's responses grew longer and less sad as the weeks passed. By Christmas Eve, mourning was officially over. Papa had to work preparing the meat for the feasting that night, and Toby and I went with him. We knew the palace would be full of fun and cheer, a welcome change after so much grief. Master Thaddeus, the fool, was in charge of the celebration as the Lord of Misrule. For twelve days before and after Christmas, he arranged the revels of the season, planning plays and mummery, games and dances.

The warmth and merriment in the kitchen was lovely, and we dodged cooks and servants as they came and went in a bustle of activity. We were too slow once, though, and a beautiful syllabub nearly went flying. At that point, Papa decided that Toby's small fingers were in danger of being chopped off accidentally, and he banished us.

We wandered through hallways draped with fir boughs and up to the nursery. There, the older princesses were readying themselves for the feast, and Prince Dickon was having his hair brushed and protesting loudly. When we entered, the girls descended on Toby, for he was a great favorite with them.

"Toby, my darling, you are growing so tall—taller than Master Niles's cakes!" cried Cecily, winking at me. She gave him a hug.

Dickon escaped from Nurse and her comb and pushed through his sisters to us. He threw an arm around Toby and pulled him away from the girls.

"Let us leave these women!" he commanded as we hooted with laughter at his childish haughtiness, and the two ran off together to play.

Bess and Cecily were old enough to join in the festivities now—saltarello dancing, sitting at the high table, eating roast goose and drinking wine—but the little princesses, Anne, Catherine, and Bridget, came with me and the boys to our old spot in the gallery. Below us Master Thaddeus sat in the king's great chair in his red-and-yellow tunic and belled cap. He commanded the lords and ladies to walk beneath the kissing bush, the ladies blushing and laughing as the gentlemen took their kisses. I scanned the crowd for Richard of Gloucester, but he wasn't there, and I was glad of it.

The mummers had just begun their acrobatics when a messenger entered the hall and bowed before King Edward, who sat at the far end of the table in Master Thaddeus's usual spot. A moment later there was a bellow from the king.

" 'Sblood!" he shouted, stilling the mummers' gaiety. "*Louis shall pay for this!*"

I watched his face redden to near purple as he threw down the parchment he'd been handed. Master Thaddeus ran over, took it up, and read it quickly. Then he turned to the company.

"A poem," he said. "Titled 'Love is Foiled, Christmas Spoiled.'" He bowed with a flourish and began to recite a verse he was obviously making up on the spot.

"The King of France
Doth take a chance
By jilting Edward's girl;
Alas for love,
But saints above—
That dauphin is a churl!"

For a moment the room was utterly silent as people waited to see if the king would laugh at the rhyme. But he did not. His face grim, he strode from the room, leaving the celebrants shocked and silent. Someone took up the parchment, and quickly whispers began.

It took only a few moments for a passing servant to bring the news up to us: Princess Bess had been jilted. King Louis of France had decided his son would do better to marry an

Austrian princess. The royal wedding between Bess and the dauphin was off.

The night ended quickly after that, with poor Bess fleeing the banquet in tears and the king storming through the palace in a terrible fury. Toby and I made our way home, trailing behind Papa through the suddenly crowded streets. Rumors of war with France were already passing through Westminster, for Bess's rejection was a terrible insult to King Edward. I wondered what this would mean for Ned. Would he return to be guardian of the realm again while his father fought? Or was Ned, now twelve as I was, old enough to go to war himself?

I fingered the gold ring that always hung at my neck, and shuddered at the idea.

· ● ·

There was no war. Before troops could be gathered, the king was taken ill.

Some said he'd caught a chill while carousing in town; others that he'd eaten a bad oyster, or a suspicious mushroom. We heard he could only lie upon his left side, that his legs were paralyzed, that he couldn't speak. Everyone had heard something different—and everyone had an opinion on what should be done for him.

As the weeks passed, all we really knew was that he was very sick indeed. Toby was not allowed in when he tried to visit Dickon nor I when I tried to see Cecily, and Papa could report only that physicians and barber-surgeons streamed in and out of the palace.

On the morning of April ninth in the year of Our Lord 1483, I woke early, uneasy in spirit and mind, though I did not know why. The sky outside my window was unbroken gray. In the courtyard our hens and rooster didn't cackle and crow, and the street was strangely quiet.

I went out through the shop, and looked up and down the empty roadway. There was not a person nor a horse-cart in sight. The ordinary noises of a Westminster morning—the clatter of hooves on cobblestones, the curses of workmen, the shouts of children playing in the street—were all absent. There was only the whisper of the river breeze blowing salty off the Thames.

For a minute, as I stood bewildered, the whole city seemed to hold its breath, and then I heard the great bell of Westminster Abbey toll once, twice, thrice. On the third note, the bells of St. Margaret's joined it, and then all the bells of Westminster and of London rang out together. It was a terrible sound, music without melody, so loud the very houses seemed to shudder with it. Heads showed through windows and open doors, and along the streets passed the news that I had already guessed:

The king! The king is dead!

Tears ran down my cheeks, and my legs shook as the great cacophony of bells and voices rose around me, and I think I would have collapsed if Papa had not come up behind me and put his strong arms around me.

The king is dead! Long live the king!

I turned my tear-streaked face up to Papa as those words reached me. "Long live the king?"

He nodded. "The new King Edward," he said softly, so I could barely hear him. "King Edward the Fifth."

Understanding slowly dawned on me.

King Edward the Fifth. Ned. My prince.

CHAPTER SEVEN

King Edward's body was laid out in Westminster Abbey. Papa was permitted to join the throngs of mourners who filed past to pay their respects. He was an esteemed man now—a member of the Worshipful Company of Butchers, the butchers' guild, and of the powerful Guild of the Assumption of the Virgin Mary, a civic guild, as well as a worker in royal service.

"The lord mayor of London was there," Papa reported to Toby and me that evening, "and all the bishops of the land, and all the nobles you have ever seen. Not a one was dry-eyed." He shook his head wearily. "There was talk of poison. How else, they say, could a strong man of forty be struck down so?"

I handed him a cup of wine and took his rain-spattered cloak from him.

"Do you believe it was poison?" I asked bluntly.

"Nay, Nell, I do not," he replied, moving to the warmth of the hall fire. "Not that there weren't those who wanted the king dead. What ruler doesn't have enemies? But King Edward was . . . not moderate, and I think it was his manner of living that killed him. God rest his soul." He made the sign of the cross, and Toby and I did too.

"God rest his soul," I repeated. "And what of Ne—what of Prince Edward? Did you hear talk of him?"

Papa sighed. "Some say that his uncle Richard of Gloucester was made protector in the late king's will."

I stared at him. Richard of Gloucester? That horrid man?

"Protector," Toby said. "What's that?"

"When a king is too young to rule, someone older and wiser is appointed to help him—a regent. And Ned is but twelve years old," Papa explained.

"Then he's not king?" Toby said, confused.

"He is king in name, but nothing else is certain. It depends on King Edward's wishes, if he made them clear. Richard may be regent and thus true ruler of the realm until Ned is old enough to be crowned properly."

"But if Ned is too young to rule, when would he become old enough?" I asked.

Papa shrugged. "There is no law about it. Perhaps when he is fourteen, perhaps sixteen. The king will have left instructions."

"Was Gloucester there? At the funeral?"

"No," Papa said. "He is up north, in York. But I've heard that he pledged his fealty to the new king at Yorkminster when he heard of his brother's death."

"That's good, then," I said. But I wasn't convinced that Richard of Gloucester's promise of loyalty could be trusted.

We stared into the fire a long time that evening, each lost in our thoughts. Even Toby was quiet. I thought of Ned, alone and far away at Ludlow, his father dead, with only his uncle Lord Rivers to turn to for reassurance and advice. What comfort could there be from a man who wore a hair shirt beneath his doublet? I knew Ned must be lonely and very afraid.

I was sure no letter I wrote would get to him, so I wrote in my book of secrets instead:

My dear Ned, I am so sorry for your terrible loss. My heart aches for you. I hope your uncle holds you close and keeps you safe. I miss you. I miss you.

· ● ·

The next day rumors swirled, as they always did in Westminster. Some said Ned was coming back from Wales; some insisted Richard of Gloucester was on his way to the city instead. There was so much uncertainty. Papa decided to go out to learn what he could, and he left with strict instructions to Toby and me to remain indoors.

As we waited for Papa's return, Toby and I wandered the house distractedly. The butcher shop was closed, as were all the shops that lined King Street and the alleys that branched off it. The street itself did not feel safe, for the gossip that floated on the air made folk nervous and prickly, and the crowds were great. We heard more than one argument turn into a fistfight outside our door. Toby begged to go out and watch, but I refused to let him.

"There's danger out there today," I warned.

He made a face. "Oh, Nell, you're an old mother hen. If a fight started, I'd just come home."

"No," I insisted. "I've heard tell of riots during the wars with Lancaster, when women and children were trampled or run through. That could happen now."

Toby snorted his disbelief, but he obeyed, for he was a good, thoughtful boy. At last Papa came back. I ran to him, demanding to know what he had learned. His face was tired and drawn, and the lines around his eyes and mouth seemed deeper. The king's death had affected him strongly.

"Apparently the king issued a new will on his deathbed," he told me. "He has indeed made Richard of Gloucester the protector."

"Oh no!" I cried. I saw Richard of Gloucester's sharp, crowlike features in my mind, felt again his hand grasping my arm.

Papa went on. "The queen and her Woodville relatives are furious. They want Ned to rule alone as king, and claim that Gloucester has no rights. And the leaders of the Guild of the Assumption of Mary say that only Parliament can choose a protector. They report that Ned—King Edward—plans to come to Westminster in May to be crowned."

"Does Ned not want his uncle to be protector, then?" I asked, for once he was properly crowned, Ned would have no need for a protector.

Papa paced the long room, stroking his beard nervously. "Who can say? Either he rejects Gloucester, or the queen does—or perhaps Lord Rivers, as the queen's brother and a Woodville, has urged this move."

Our maid, Demelza, hurried into the room. Her usually placid face was worried. "Master Gould!" she said. "I can't find Toby. He is nowhere in the house."

"Did you look in the shop?" I asked anxiously. "Or the solar? Has Simon seen him?"

"I searched everywhere," Demelza assured me. "Simon has been down to Bell's Inn these past two days, drinking with the other journeymen. To be sure, Toby's not with him."

Papa and I exchanged a panicked look. "I'd best search for him," Papa said. "I'll go up and down King Street and check the alleys. You and Demelza stay here in case he returns. Have you any idea where he might go, Nell?"

"He said he wanted to go out," I said helplessly.

"Then out I will go in search of him," Papa told me, and ran out the door. As soon as he was well away, I grabbed my cloak and hurried out myself, ignoring Demelza's protests.

Outside seemed a solid mass of people, shoving and shouting. All those who ordinarily would be working were out on the street, clustered in groups or moving aimlessly over the cobblestones. Horses tried to push through the throng, their riders calling out, "*Ho, there!*" and "*Move on, you!*" Harsh replies greeted these shouts. I saw a mounted nobleman reach down with a gloved hand and cuff a lad who refused to move from his path. It was only because his friends forcibly restrained him that the boy did not pull the lord from his horse to be beaten on the street below.

I darted through the crowd frantically, calling, "*Toby! Toby Gould!*" at the top of my voice. I asked Mistress Kendall the flaxwife and Master Niles the baker if they had seen him, but they had not. As I passed one couple, I overheard them arguing, and their words drew me up in fear.

"If Richard is to be king, the princes will have to go," the man said. "Edward and Dickon both." He wobbled on his feet, clearly under the influence of drink.

"Hush, husband!" the woman hissed. "That be treason!"

"Is it so?" her husband said. "Then Richard must drown me in a butt of malmsey like he did his own brother!"

When they saw me staring, the woman bared her teeth in a snarl, and I rushed onward. Finally I reached the palace gates, where armed guards stood to keep the people out.

"Have you seen my brother Toby, the son of the king's butcher? A boy of seven, with brown hair?" I asked, near tears.

"Brown hair and a dirty face?" one of the guards said. "Aye, an urchin like that did dodge right past us an hour ago. Nay, mistress, no one is allowed—"

I ran past him and into the outer courtyard. Behind me, the guard shouted, "*If you ask me, the both of ye need a good whipping!*"

The palace seemed strangely quiet after the tumult of the street. Ordinarily, the halls and courtyards would be swarming with people—servants, merchants, courtiers. Now the glass windows winked emptily, and the hallways were unguarded and deserted. Near the vast kitchens I ran into Master Thaddeus, though I barely recognized him. He wasn't in his fool's motley.

To my surprise, I was now taller than he; I hadn't realized how very short and thin he was.

"Master Thaddeus!" I cried. "It's Nell, Nell Gould. Do you remember me?"

The fool's eyes narrowed as he examined me, but then recognition dawned. " 'Tis the butcher's daughter, is it not? What are you doing here? This is no good day to be at court."

"I'm looking for my brother—he's run off. Have you seen him? Toby Gould, playmate of Prince Richard—Dickon?"

Master Thaddeus shook his head. "Nay, child, I've seen almost no one this last day. All the royal family have gone to the Tower. I'm to join the queen there till young King Edward's coronation—if there is a coronation."

"What do you mean, '*if* there is a coronation'?"

The fool smiled, but the smile didn't reach his eyes. "There is a dark spider that sits in the North, weaving his web and waiting for his supper."

His words made me nervous, and my nerves made me angry. "Speak clearly!" I demanded. "I've no time for riddles!"

Master Thaddeus knit his brows together and scowled, and suddenly it was as if Richard of Gloucester's face glared out at me. I gasped and stepped back. Then he smiled, and his supple face was his own again.

"I must get to the queen, for you know she cannot rule without me. Mistress Nell, I hope that we shall meet again. Beware of dukes!" He bowed, turned, and was gone, leaving me bewildered and even more fearful than I had been before.

There is a dark spider that sits in the North. . . . He meant Richard, who sat up north in his city of York, fuming, as Ned planned to leave Ludlow and start for London to claim his throne. Did Ned know? I wondered. Did he know that his uncle might be a threat to him?

I shook my head, remembering why I was there. I left the kitchens and ran up the stairs and through the halls to the nursery. I passed precious few servants. A palpable air of tension filled the stone corridors and high-ceilinged rooms, and I hoped the comforting familiarity of the nursery would dispel it.

The room, like the rest of the palace, was unusually neat and empty. Toys were put away, beds were made; the table was free of crumbs. But the warmth of the place remained. I could almost see the children tumbling about, myself among them, Nurse laughing at our antics and Lady Mistress Darcy scolding us for dirtying our clothes. I closed my eyes and breathed in the nursery smell of milk and clean linen, and then I heard a soft hiccup coming from a corner of the room.

"Who's there?" I asked sharply, my nerves on edge.

I strode to the corner, where an oaken cupboard stood. The hiccup came again, and I pulled open the cupboard door. Toby's tear-stained face looked up at me beseechingly.

In a flash I forgot my worry and my anger. I pulled him out and hugged him tight, feeling his soft cheek against mine.

"What are you doing here, Toby?" I demanded. "We've been worried to death!"

Toby snuffled and wiped his nose on his sleeve, turning his

head from me in embarrassment. I knew what he was thinking—a big boy like him, crying like a baby!

"I wanted to see Dickon," he admitted. "I heard people talking in the street—they said terrible things. I needed to warn him."

"Oh, Toby," I said limply. How could I fault him for having the same impulse I'd had? "You're a brave, foolish boy, do you know that? The queen, the princesses, Dickon—they've all gone to the Tower. Could there be any safer place?"

We had seen the Tower of London from a distance many times, its thick protective walls surrounding strong, square buildings. The Tower was where kings went to await coronation . . . and where traitors went to await execution. It was a fortress.

"They're all there?" Toby asked.

"All but Ned, for he's in Ludlow still."

"And is Ned in danger?"

There was no avoiding Toby's straightforward question, and I gave him an honest answer. "I think he may be. It's not the same for him as for them. Kings have more enemies than anyone."

Toby nodded and moved out of my embrace. "Then we must say a prayer for his safekeeping."

I looked at my brother, his sweet freckled face and wide blue eyes, and I loved him more than ever at that moment. He had tried to do what he could to help; now he would place the new king in God's hands. And I could only do the same.

CHAPTER EIGHT

On the night of April thirtieth, a great tumult began in the streets.
Toby heard it first and ran into my room, his eyes wide with fear.

"Nell, wake up! There's a horrible loud noise outside! What's happening?"

I sat up in bed and listened. The roaring of many voices reached me, and I threw a furred robe over my nightdress and sprang up.

"Come!" I said to Toby. We met Papa downstairs in the hall and rushed to the front window. I gasped to see the crush of people in the street, some holding torches that threw a wild, flickering light onto the faces of the crowd.

"Henry!" Papa called through the window to a man in the street, and Master Henton, the armorer, came toward us.

"John!" he cried. "A more evil night there never was! Do you know the news?"

"What's happened?" Papa demanded.

"The Duke of Gloucester has taken the king prisoner! Lord Rivers is arrested!"

Papa stiffened. *"By the saints!"* he swore. "I didn't think he would do it!"

"The queen has fled from the Tower by the river way to sanctuary," Master Henton continued. "Now she sits in a daze and cannot move. She fears for her life, so they say, and the lives of her sons!"

"Oh, Papa," I whispered in disbelief. Ned was a prisoner, and his uncle arrested? How could this happen? Papa put one arm around me and the other around Toby. We stood like that just outside the shop till dawn, as the crowd moved and moaned like a single living thing and rumors and terror flew wild around us. I wrote the worst of what I heard in my book of secrets:

Will there be another War of the Roses—only this one white rose against white? Richard against Ned? Will we be plunged into chaos and death again, with brother fighting brother and all of us the losers?

Richard of Gloucester set out from York for London three days later, but before he did, he wrote to the lord mayor to calm his fears. This letter was read to a meeting of the Guild of the Assumption, which Papa attended, and he reported its contents to me.

"Gloucester said he did not imprison the king but rescued him from Lord Rivers, so as to save the realm. It's a lie. It's treachery!" Papa fumed, pacing before the fire. He took a cup of wine from Demelza and spun on his heel, spilling most upon the oak floor. "He says he and the king will come to the city for the coronation, and all at the meeting believed it. But I don't believe it. The Duke of Gloucester wants the crown for himself."

I wiped up the spilled wine, my hand shaking. Poor Ned! I thought of the old rumors about the murders of King Henry and the Duke of Clarence. What if Richard of Gloucester *had* killed those men—one an anointed king, the other his own brother? What would prevent him from killing his nephew now, with the crown of England as a prize?

· • ·

On May the fourth, the date originally set for Ned's coronation, we went down the Strand to London to watch the arrival of Ned and Richard of Gloucester. The sun shone brilliantly down on the crowd, but there was no feeling of gaiety or joy. I stood in the silent throng as the procession approached.

First came the lord mayor and the aldermen, all in scarlet tunics, and behind them rode a group of three. Ned sat astride in the center, dressed in blue velvet, his face pale and set, his gold curls dancing in the breeze. On one side of him rode Richard of Gloucester, and on the other side the Duke of Buckingham, Richard's close friend, both dressed in somber black. Behind them stretched a line of hundreds of armed soldiers. I stared at Ned, willing him to see me, but his gaze was fixed before him—fixed, I think, so he would not weep.

But Richard turned to the crowd and made a sweeping gesture with his arm toward Ned. He called, "Behold, your prince and sovereign lord, saved from the treasonous Lord Rivers!" Again he cried this, and the crowd began to cheer as tears ran down my face. I knew it was a lie. How could the people believe that he meant no harm to their prince? Did they not see how Ned was caught, trapped between these men of evil intentions?

The crowd dispersed peacefully after that, and we went home feeling dismal and worried. I tried to ease my fears by writing them down.

He seems so alone. Oh Ned! Are you afraid? What will you do? What will they do to you? All our talk about your dread of being king—was this what you feared? Did you ever think your own uncle would betray you? The way he gripped my arm that day, the way he bruised and hurt me—and I was nothing to him, no threat, no challenge. He wants to be king, and you are in his way. How will he grip and squeeze and hurt you?

Master Caxton stopped by that evening, and he and Papa talked long into the night, drinking spiced wine and staring gloomily into the fire. Toby and I stood quietly just beyond the door, unable to sleep, listening.

"Gloucester has set abroad a rumor that the queen's family intend to murder him," Master Caxton reported. "He maintains that the Woodvilles want him out of the way to ensure their own power. And he is trying to get the council to agree that Lord Rivers has committed treason. He claims the man wants the throne for himself."

"That's madness," Papa said, shaking his head. "Everyone knows that Rivers would never act against Ned—against King Edward."

"The council will not condemn Rivers," Master Caxton agreed. "But Gloucester must get rid of him and break the queen's family in order to seize the crown. He will find a way."

"Though I have tried to, I never trusted Gloucester," Papa admitted quietly. "He's the sort that lurks in corners and listens in on conversations."

Master Caxton gave a sad little laugh, and behind the door, I nodded. Papa didn't know how right he was.

Toby could stay still no longer. "What of Dickon?" he cried, pulling me into the room. "Is the prince in danger?"

"Why are you still awake?" Papa snapped. "You should be abed, the both of you."

"But—Dickon!" Toby insisted. "What will happen to him?"

"Prince Dickon is safe as long as the king his brother lives," Papa said shortly. "Now go to bed."

We left the hall silently, and I took Toby's hand on the stairs.

"As long as the king lives," Toby repeated in a low voice. "Nell, what does Papa mean? Would the Duke of Gloucester dare to kill Ned? Could he do that?"

I had never lied to my brother, and I didn't want to start now.

"I don't know what men are capable of doing," I said tiredly. "God alone can tell. I just don't know, Toby. Terrible things have been done to win the crown before."

We changed into our nightclothes, and Toby slept in my room, lying in the little trundle bed where he had spent nights as a baby stricken with stomach pains or the ear-ache. As on those nights, we slumbered little. I heard Toby turning and turning as the slow hours passed, and I tossed about myself, thinking of Ned imprisoned in luxury in the Bishop's Palace at St. Paul's, not knowing how his family fared nor what would happen to him on the morrow.

The days passed for me in an agony of waiting. All of England waited with me, for no one knew what the Duke of Gloucester had planned.

After a week the Royal Council met, and from what we heard, the meeting was entirely controlled by Richard. It was decided that Ned would move to the Tower, where he would await his coronation—now set for June the twenty-fourth. Lord Hastings, who had always been a supporter of King Edward and of Ned—and who had taught the princesses and me archery when we were small—allowed Gloucester to be made protector. Richard was now officially in control of the realm.

"Papa," I asked when we heard of this, "why would Lord Hastings support Gloucester over Ned?" He had been King Edward's most trusted advisor. Why would he suddenly switch sides?

Papa gave the sigh that had become customary with him. "It goes back a long way, Nell," he said. "Lord Hastings has always despised the queen's family, and his hatred is returned by them in full; their ambitions have often been at odds. Some have said—though I don't believe it—that the queen was jealous of Hastings, for his close friendship with the late king. They say that on his deathbed King Edward commanded Hastings to be friendly with the Woodvilles, so as to try to settle things between them."

I nodded. So many people hated the Woodvilles for being upstarts. King Edward had given them titles and lands and made them the most powerful family in the country, but they angered lords and commoners alike with their snobbery and greed. The whispers that they were sorcerers, even murderers, were never quiet.

"Hastings and Gloucester have always been close, because Gloucester was beloved of the king. So, as I've heard, after the king's death Lord Hastings felt he had to warn Gloucester against the Woodvilles and their influence on Ned."

"I see," I said.

"To be sure, I think Lord Hastings truly feels that a protectorate is the best thing for the kingdom. He is a loyal and trustworthy man and always has been."

"Then he'll make certain that Ned is safe," I said hopefully.

Papa was silent.

· ● ·

At the beginning of June, we went to the abbey to ask for an audience with the queen. It was Papa's idea. His loyalty had been with Her Majesty from the first, when he stepped out from the crowd to ask her needs.

As we walked through the elegant halls of the abbot's residence, Papa compared the atmosphere to that of his visits almost thirteen years earlier, before my birth.

"There are no guards for the queen now, no supporters in the hallways," he murmured. "And where are the abbot's servants? There are no fires burning in the rooms!"

"It's warm outside," I protested, but that didn't matter. We both knew that the abbot wasn't even in residence; he had left for the countryside, as he feared that Gloucester might think he supported the queen. Thirteen years ago he'd not hesitated to help her, but now, it was clear, he believed he had to flee for his life. This, more than anything I'd seen, told me the danger Ned and his family faced.

We were ushered into Queen Elizabeth's presence by a single servant. It was a different room than the one Papa had described to me when I was little. This chamber was long and narrow, with dark wooden floors and walls. The ceiling was vaulted and painted with flowers and leaves; every inch of wall that wasn't elaborately carved was hung with tapestry. It should have been a beautiful room, but there was a chill in it that wasn't just the lack of a fire in the large stone fireplace.

The queen sat near an arched window at a distance from her ladies, with only Master Thaddeus nearby. The princesses were nowhere in sight. Dickon was there, though, playing at his mother's feet. He ran to Toby with a glad cry, and the two raced into another room together. The queen turned a pale face to Papa.

"Master Gould," she said softly.

I could barely restrain a gasp as I saw how drawn, how much older she seemed. Her beauty was muted now, as late autumn leaves, though still holding a hint of their early vividness, are faded to near brown. Lines of exhaustion marred the smoothness of her cheeks and brow, and even her gold hair, unfettered by any cap, didn't shine with its usual brilliance.

"Your Majesty," Papa replied, going down on one knee and kissing her hand. "What can we do?"

"You have already done all I could ask," she told him. "That is the first time Dickon has smiled since his father died. He has been so fearful, and so lonely. . . . I should have thought earlier to summon his dearest friend." She turned to me. "Come here, child."

I came to her and went down in a curtsy, graceful now with practice.

"You have grown up, Nell."

"Yes, Your Majesty," I said.

"You are near as tall as Ned. And I was wrong about you. There is indeed some beauty in you. You will become a fine woman. You'll marry, bear children. . . . Is there a young man who interests you?"

Only Ned. "No, Your Majesty."

Master Thaddeus looked up from his book and grinned. "No suitor for such a lovely lady? No butcher, no baker, no candlestick maker?" I blushed and frowned at him, but he waggled his brows so comically that I had to smile.

The queen nodded. "Time enough for that." Her gaze passed over me, and she said, "Will Ned have time for that, I wonder? Will he marry, have children? A son who will be king after him? What think you, Mistress Gould?" Her voice was high and trembling.

"Oh, Your Majesty," I said, and my voice shook too. "Of course he will. He must!"

"He must," she repeated musingly. "If only it were that easy! But he is taken from me and imprisoned. I cannot raise an army from sanctuary. And no one dares support my son. Lord Hastings despises me, though he loved the king. Gloucester has worked swiftly, and well. I fear that my children and I face death."

"No!" Papa and I said together. I was horrified; I had never imagined the queen would yield in this way. Her strength had always been great, but with her son stolen, she bent, and broke. She could be no help to Ned, nor he to her.

"Lord Hastings loves your son as he did his father," Papa reminded her. "He won't let any harm come to him."

"Do you truly believe that, Master Gould?" the queen asked. I could hear both desperation and hope in her voice.

"I do, Your Majesty. He has always had young King Edward's best interests at heart."

The queen sighed and nodded. "We must trust him, I suppose. He is all we have."

We stayed an hour and had a meal, very plain and simple—bread, an eel pie, and wine. Papa tried to cheer the queen with stories of King Street, and Master Thaddeus told riddles.

"My life can be measured in hours,

I serve by being devoured.

Thin, I am swift; fat, I am slow;

And always wind is my foe," he recited, and quickly I guessed, "A candle!"

The queen had drifted off someplace within her mind and paid us little heed. We took our leave at last, and the boys wept at being parted.

"Will you bring Toby again?" the queen asked Papa. "He is such a comfort to Dickon."

"Of course, Your Majesty," Papa assured her. "And I shall supply you with the best meats, for your kitchen seems a bit . . . depleted." He looked pointedly at the dishes on the table.

"Alas," said Master Thaddeus. "What is the point of being queen if the food is bad? Bring us pheasant and duck—smuggle in some good luck!"

"No, you should not bring any food." The queen's voice was weary. "If word gets out that you have helped us . . ."

Papa snorted angrily. "That did not stop me before, and it shall not stop me now!"

The queen rose, and smiled, but the smile did not reach

her eyes. "You are a good man, Butcher Gould. God bless you for your kindness to me and my family." Papa kissed her hand again and we left, walking silently through the empty halls, our only company our own bleak thoughts.

A few days later we returned, bearing fine cuts of kid and lamb and beef that Papa thought suitable for a queen in distress. I brought my mending, for I planned to stay some hours to give Toby and Dickon time to play.

I went directly to the dark wood-paneled room. The queen was not in her seat by the arched window, and her ladies were not in evidence, but Princess Cecily sat before the cold hearth with her needlework, and I curtseyed to her.

"I'm terribly sorry about your father the king," I said awkwardly. It seemed a dreadful understatement, considering the circumstances. Cecily brushed away tears, dropped her embroidery, and stood to hug me tightly.

"Don't curtsy to me," she scolded me. "We're still who we were—though I suppose I am less than what I was!" She motioned to her gloomy surroundings, and I nodded.

"This must be horrid for you," I said. "To be closed in here like a prisoner . . ."

"It's comfortable, at least," Cecily said. "And we are together. I am so frightened for Ned, though. And Mother—she can't sleep at night, or if she does sleep, she wakes with screaming nightmares. She is very unwell this morning—her head aches terribly."

"Oh, Cecily!" I couldn't think of anything that could console her.

"Did you know the abbot himself has run away? Mother was furious. 'That fat frocked coward,' she called him."

I bit my lip to keep from smiling. That sounded more like the queen.

We settled ourselves with our needlework. Cecily, usually so happy, was quiet and anxious, and asked nothing about life beyond the abbey walls. There was hardly any sound but the muted voices of Toby and Dickon from the next room.

After an hour or so, we heard a great hubbub outside the room, the sounds of boots and of metal clashing. We sprang up, our needlework falling to the floor, and Cecily turned wide, terrified eyes to me. A moment later, Papa came running from the kitchens, and from another doorway Queen Elizabeth appeared. If she suffered from headache, it didn't show. Her back was straight and her expression grim.

"Where are the boys?" she demanded. Her strength seemed returned to her. "Bring me the prince!"

A maidservant hurried out of the room and came back a moment later with Dickon and Toby. Behind them the other princesses were clustered—Bess, Anne, Catherine, and little Bridget. Dickon's face was parchment-white, his lips quivering. The queen rushed to her son and bent to embrace him, and Toby ran to where I stood. I put my own arms around him.

"Do not forget," the queen said fiercely to Dickon. "You are your father's son, and brother to the king. Conduct yourself as you should." She pressed a kiss on his golden curls, so like his brother's.

"Children, come," Papa commanded. I reached out to squeeze Cecily's hand and then hurried to his side, Toby close beside me. We moved a ways down the corridor, stopping when we heard a crash from behind us. Papa pushed Toby onward, but I turned back to watch.

A door flew open, and a group of soldiers surged into the room we had left. There must have been thirty or more—they filled the space to bursting. Behind them I could see the tonsured heads and ashen faces of the abbey's monks, powerless to stop the armed men. The queen stood tall, her hands on Dickon's shoulders.

"You dare to violate this sanctuary, against the law of men and of God?" she cried. "You shall be cursed for your heresy!"

Some of the soldiers hesitated at that, but their leader, a tall man in burnished armor, advanced. When he stood before the queen, he removed his helmet and handed it to a soldier behind him.

"Nell, come!" Papa urged me. But I could not move.

"Your Majesty," the soldier said, bowing his head. "We are under orders from the Duke of Gloucester to remove His Highness the prince to the Tower to join his brother."

I put a hand over my mouth to hold back a gasp. Behind me in the hall, Papa and Toby had stopped and stood listening.

"I am only a woman, though I be a queen," Queen Elizabeth

replied calmly, even gently. "What can I do against an army? But you will have to take him from me, for he is my son, and I would not willingly give him over."

I had been wrong about her strength. Where her children were concerned, the queen was still sovereign.

The soldier came forward, put his own hands on Dickon's arm, and pulled him, but the queen held him tightly. Dickon stumbled, but righted himself, standing as tall as his little frame would allow. He did not cry or hide his face. His father, I thought, would have been proud.

"Let me go, Mother!" he said forcefully. "All shall be well, and I will be with my brother the king. We will take care of each other."

The queen released him, biting her lip so hard a drop of blood fell on her bodice. There were so many soldiers, and the queen was so defenseless, with her little daughters huddling behind her. Dickon moved to the soldier's side.

"The prince will not be harmed, Your Majesty," the soldier assured the queen.

"If he is," Queen Elizabeth said in that same gentle tone, "you can be sure you will suffer the torments of the damned, both before and after your death."

Even from a distance, I could see the soldier grow pale. But he did not falter. He turned away, one hand still on Dickon's narrow shoulder, and the whole troop moved out of the room, armor clanking.

There was a terrible silence, and then the queen crumpled

to the ground. Cecily and Bess ran to her, and I did too, dashing back down the corridor with Papa just behind me. We helped her to her feet, where she stood swaying.

"My sons are captive, and their uncle has the realm," Queen Elizabeth murmured. "I am alone and undone."

CHAPTER NINE

The monks came in then, and they told us the whole dreadful tale. There had been a meeting of councilors at the Tower of London, led by Lord Hastings, Ned's greatest defender. One of the monks described what he had heard about it: "Hastings and the others believed they were there to discuss King Edward's coronation. Everyone was friendly. Gloucester even brought strawberries—strawberries!"

Another monk, impatient, broke in. "They say that Gloucester went out for a time, and when he came back, he was angry. No one seems to know what happened to anger him. But straightaway he accused the men at the meeting of plotting against him."

The first monk said, "They say Gloucester was so furious that he pounded on the table as he railed against them!"

We all gasped.

"There was a struggle," the first monk continued, "and Hastings and the others were arrested on the spot."

"Someone was killed," the second monk said. "Or stabbed, at the very least."

The first monk shook his head. "That is not certain. But Gloucester told Hastings to visit a priest for last rites, and cried out, 'By St. Paul, I will not go to dinner till I see your head off!'"

The queen clasped her hands together so tightly her knuckles whitened. "And then?" she whispered.

"And then," the second monk said, his voice unsteady, "Hastings was beheaded right then in the courtyard of the Tower."

The queen stumbled to a chair and sat, her strength entirely gone.

"Lord Hastings is dead, dead!" Cecily moaned. "What will become of our brothers? What will become of us, now that we have lost our only support? Is there no one Richard will not kill?"

I tried to soothe her, but there was no real consolation I could give. I pushed back my own tears, remembering the kind man who'd joked with me years before about my lack of skill at the bow and arrow, his sympathetic touch on my shoulder. And now he was . . . beheaded. *Beheaded!* It was too awful to contemplate.

And if Richard of Gloucester was powerful enough to kill even Lord Hastings, who was loved by everyone, it seemed nothing could stop him.

We left the queen surrounded by the few ladies who had stayed with her, all of them as nervous and flighty as birds. A wild scene greeted us outside the abbey walls. Richard had sent messengers to run through the streets crying, "Treason!

Treason!" and the call was taken up by those who could be convinced of anything. King Street was filled with bewildered folk wandering aimlessly, tossing about rumors that the king had been murdered, that the Bishop of Ely was dead, that Hastings had been executed. Only the last was true, but no one knew what to believe.

We pushed through the crowds to our house and shut ourselves inside, sore at heart over this latest evidence that Richard indeed plotted to steal the throne for himself.

I had no word from Ned in all this time, but I knew now that he was a prisoner and so would not be permitted to write or contact anyone. No sooner had we reached the house, though, when there came a knock on our door, and I opened it to find a man I had never seen before, wrapped in a dark cloak.

"Mistress Gould?" he inquired, and when I nodded, he thrust a small leather pouch at me, turned, and was gone before I could ask a single question. I looked at the pouch carefully, but it held no hint of its sender, so I opened it and slid the contents into my palm.

It was my ring, the moonstone I had given to Ned.

I fell back, slamming the door, weak and faint with fear. What was it I had said to him, up in the gallery? *If you ever need me, send this. I will come to you.*

I took the ring to Papa and stood before him, anxious and shaken. "From Ned," I whispered.

"What does this mean? You have exchanged rings with the king?" he asked me sternly, tilting my head up with his hand and looking into my eyes. I am sure he expected me to look away, or to blush, but I did neither. I merely nodded, feeling no shame.

"Yes," I admitted, pulling out Ned's gold ring from my bodice. "But we didn't plight our troth with these rings. They were a promise to each other of help if ever we should need it. Ned knew trouble would come; I think he has always known it. But Papa, how can I go to him? And if I went, what could I do for him?"

Papa shook his head and began the pacing that had become habit with him. "I can think of nothing, child. You have no power, no connections. The only help you could give him is comfort."

I started to cry. "Maybe that's all he wants from me. And if it is, how could I refuse him?"

"No!" Papa said. "It is too dangerous for you. And it is an impossibility. The Duke of Gloucester would never let anyone into the Tower to see the king."

"No?" I said softly, wiping the tears from my cheeks. "Not even a butcher's daughter, a girl of no consequence?"

Papa paused in his pacing and looked hard at me. I could see the war being waged inside his mind: on the one side, his long years of loyalty to King Edward and the queen, his horror at the Duke of Gloucester's schemes; on the other, his love for his only daughter and his fear for my safety.

Finally he shook his head. He had no workable plan, nor did I. There was nothing we could do.

"May the good Lord help them all," Papa said, and we sank

to our knees to pray for the safety of the two princes, alone and imprisoned by their uncle's hand.

· ● ·

Two nights later, we were summoned to the queen.

Something in me had been expecting this. Before we left, I took my moonstone ring and slipped it into a pouch at my waist, and I checked to be sure that Ned's ring was in its place about my neck.

We walked the streets of Westminster in the uneasy dark. Toby's hand was clammy in mine. There was silence now, the crowds abed for a few hours before they gathered again to resume their endless speculation and accusation. There was no guard at the abbey at all, and I asked Papa why.

"There is nothing left to guard," he said shortly, and I shivered, pulling my cape around me to shut out the night chill.

The queen sat alone in the same cold, narrow room, still as death, on a straight wooden chair. Her black dress was immaculate, but her hair was unbound and uncovered, for there were no servants to dress it. Her head was bowed, and she did not raise it when we entered. Papa went to her and dropped to one knee, kissing her hand that lay limply on the chair arm.

"Your Majesty," he said. Then he could think of nothing more.

"Your Majesty, where are the princesses? And Master Thaddeus?" I asked at last. I couldn't imagine that the fool would leave his queen.

"The girls are resting. I have sent Master Thaddeus to his

people," the queen replied tonelessly. "He raged and stormed, but I ordered it, and he could not disobey me."

She said nothing more, nor did we. Silence lay over us, though silence in that great abbey was never true quiet. The ancient walls creaked and groaned, settling their old bones ever deeper in the earth, and mice scratched and scurried from place to place. The wind whistled at times through the ill-fitting windows and down the chimneys. But there was no sound from the princesses, no chatter of attendants in the outer rooms. Where the queen was, there had always been noise and activity, and now there was none.

More than anything, it was the silence that told me she was queen no longer.

At last she looked up at us. Her eyes glittered, though I could not tell if it was with tears or with a burning anger.

"Richard of Gloucester has both my sons. The line of Edward is extinct."

"Oh no!" I cried. I couldn't stop myself. "They are alive, Your Majesty. As long as they still live, you must hope!"

She turned to me, and the light in her eyes went out—they were dull and lifeless. "My dear," she said, "Gloucester would not allow me to send any attendants to my sons, nor would he allow me to go to them myself. But he did grant me one boon, and that boon means asking a favor of you, so great a favor that you must not hesitate to deny me if you choose."

What could she possibly mean? I couldn't imagine ever denying the queen anything. She held over my family the same power she always had, and I knew we would do whatever she wanted.

"Master Gould, stand," she ordered Papa. "My favor is hardest on you, so of you I will ask it first. Now listen. I have asked Gloucester, and he has agreed that my sons may have a companion, someone to—to 'play with,' as he put it. I told him that I knew of a brother and sister, old playmates of the princes, children of a butcher in town. He knows you, it seems, or knows of you. He thought about the idea for a time, twisting it and turning it to see how a butcher's children could be a threat to him, but even Gloucester, who sees a conspiracy in every corner, could see none there. So he has granted me this indulgence, that Nell and Toby may go to the Tower, there to stay for a time with my sons the king and Prince Dickon."

We were all speechless. What did it mean, to stay in the Tower with the boys? Would we, too, be prisoners?

The queen must have read my questions on my face, for she answered me. "You would not be able to come and go as you pleased. I do not know how much your movements would be restricted, but you would be watched and guarded, I am sure. I believe you would be able to send word out to your father, though your letters would be read and censored.

"For Gloucester, you see, your stay with the princes would look very well. The public would be sure to hear of it, as that sort of news passes through the streets more quickly and easily than the river breeze. They would take it as a sign of his good intentions toward the boys." Her tone was flat and uninflected.

Papa tried to speak, but the words caught in his throat.

"Your Majesty," he managed finally. "If your sons are at risk, then would my children not also be in danger?"

The queen pressed her hands together as if in prayer. "I think not, Master Gould. Truly, I believe that if Gloucester meant to . . . to *harm* the princes, he would not do so with witnesses. I know he is a vicious man, but his viciousness always has reason, and he does not want to turn the people against himself. I think that as long as your children are with mine, mine are safe. Mine are still alive."

I thought of the Duke of Gloucester's iron grip on my arm that day in the Great Hall, of his fierce, dark gaze boring into me. Did he remember me, even now? I doubted that he forgot anything. He knew I was nobody. As a witness, I wouldn't matter to him.

But still, the idea of being with Ned, of helping him . . .

Papa bowed his head. I could not see his face, but I could imagine the turmoil that he must have felt. The queen, whom he loved and had always obeyed, had asked him to put his children in danger. How could he answer? I saw his hands clench, saw a throbbing in the side of his jaw, and I thought I would help him to settle the matter.

"Papa, if it would aid the prince and king, we would like to go," I said.

I turned at once to Toby, as I had spoken for him. He nodded.

"My dear," Papa said. He raised his head, eyes glistening with tears. "Do you know what you say?"

I thought I did. That night, I truly thought that I could

face the danger. I told myself that we would be safe. I forced myself to believe it.

I took Papa's hand in mine and held it, rough and work-worn, to my cheek. "We can lighten their burden, Papa. If we could do that, then we must go. Am I not right?"

Papa's hand, cold as ice, closed around mine. "It may be that you could lighten their burden, Nell, but I cannot allow it," he said, his voice breaking. "Your Majesty, you know I would do anything for you—almost anything. But these are my children. I cannot let them go."

There was a silence. Then the queen straightened herself and said, "Master Gould, if I commanded you, would you send them?"

Papa stood stock still. I could see the shock in his eyes, and I felt it myself. It seemed like a very long time passed before he answered.

"You are my queen," he said. "I will obey you in every way I can. But this I cannot do, even at my own peril."

The queen did not seem surprised. She merely nodded, and then turned her head away from us. It was clear we were dismissed.

I was angry on the walk back down King Street—furious, in fact. I had made a promise to Ned to come if he needed me, as he had made the same promise to me, and Papa was making me break it. Ned *needed* me, and I could not go to him. It seemed the greatest unfairness in the world. But Papa's word was law.

I sat in my room as the sun rose, fuming. When Demelza knocked to announce breakfast, I refused to come down. I knew that I was acting like a child, but I felt that I had been treated like one.

Toby came in after breakfast and perched on my bed, handing me a hunk of bread. I ate a little, but I wasn't very hungry. My stomach roiled from anger and worry.

"What if we snuck out after bedtime?" he ventured after a time. "We could go to the Tower without anyone knowing."

I was surprised, for Toby nearly always minded Papa without argument. Like me, though, he was torn between his friend and his father, his queen and his father. Who was right? Who should be obeyed?

I had considered his idea already. "What would happen when we got to the Tower, though? The guards would laugh at us and turn us away. They'd have no reason to let us in."

Toby thought about this and nodded reluctantly. "Yes. I see."

I reached over and squeezed his hand. "It's lovely that you to want to help Dickon," I said. "But I can think of no way to do it."

As we sat, lost in our dark thoughts, there came a loud pounding on the front door. We heard the creak as Demelza opened it, and then a cry from her and the clanking of armor. Startled, we looked at each other, then ran for the stairs.

In the hall we found a group of armed men facing Papa, who stood protectively in front of a cowering Demelza. "What is this intrusion?" Papa demanded.

"Master Gould, we come at the instruction of the queen and the lord protector. We have orders to bring your children to the Tower."

Papa drew in a sharp breath. "Are—are they arrested?" he managed.

"No, sir," the soldier replied. "They are to be companions to the young princes. They shall be lodged in comfort. No harm will come to them."

"And this is the lord protector's wish—or the queen's?"

"I do not know, Master Butcher. The order is signed by both."

I looked at Papa. His face was pale and unreadable. I couldn't imagine what he was feeling. The queen he had served for so long, at such risk to his own safety and that of his family, had betrayed him—and had gone to Richard of Gloucester to do it. I know now that it must have been agonizing for him to realize that he had become nothing more to her than a means to an end.

I took Toby's hand in mine. "May we pack some things to take with us?" I asked. I was proud that my voice was steady.

"Pack swiftly," the soldier commanded.

I turned to Papa and said, "It will be all right. We will be careful, I promise."

Oh, I was such a child. God forgive me.

Demelza and I piled clothing and warm blankets and food into leather satchels. I put my book of secrets in my pocket, in case the guards searched our bags. When we were nearly finished, another knock came on the door. I ran downstairs, pulled the heavy oaken door open, and was startled to see Master Caxton and Jacob standing in the dim daylight. Papa must have sent Simon to fetch them, I realized.

Papa and Master Caxton spoke privately for a few minutes. Then Papa took me aside. "If we are able to get permission, Master Caxton will send Jacob to the Tower once each week with a few books so the king can keep up with his studies and you can have some amusement," he told me in a low voice. "That way, Jacob will be able to tell me how you fare." His jaw was set. I had rarely seen my father angry, but he was angry now—and at the queen.

I nodded and went back upstairs to finish packing my satchel. A sound behind me made me jump, and I saw that Jacob had followed me up the stairs. He crossed the room quickly to where I stood and placed his hands on my shoulders, turning me toward him. I tried to pull away, but he held me fast.

"Nell, you should not do this," he said in a low voice. "You do not know the danger. Your father should not let you do this."

"I do know the danger!" I protested. "And you can't blame Papa. He forbade us to go. We are taken against his will—what could he do? Really, Jacob, let me go!"

"And is it against your will as well?"

I didn't answer.

"Nell, if anything happened to you . . ." Jacob's hands loosened on my shoulders, and he turned away, but I saw the look in his eyes before he did. I stared at his back, broad as a man's, in astonishment. Jacob was nearly fifteen now, a journeyman, and would soon be a printer in his own right. He would be of an age to choose a wife. It had never occurred to me before that he might think of me in that way, and I didn't know what to make of the idea. My mind was so crowded with worry, fear, excitement—I could not even entertain the thought of love.

"Jacob," I began, but he turned back to me before I could finish.

"I know we're young still, Nell," he said. "I would wait for you, if you'd give me encouragement to wait. No—don't answer now. I will see you every week, I hope, when I bring the books. We'll talk then, if we have the chance. But think on it, Nell. Will you?"

I nodded, completely befuddled. He took my hand and kissed it gently, and then he turned and left the room.

I stared after him blindly, thinking of his familiar face—his large brown eyes, his chin with the hint of a dimple in it. Could that be the face of a husband? I replayed the scene in my mind, but it still seemed too strange to believe. Jacob and I had worked together for years, and never once had he shown me any attention but that which an elder brother might show to his sister. But all along, perhaps, he had been seeing me in a different light. For just a moment, I imagined a life with him: a little print shop with cozy rooms above. A child, or two.

Papa called me from downstairs, and I woke from my reverie. I pushed the thought of Jacob away for the time; I would have to consider it later. In the Tower, I would have time to think.

Master Caxton went back to his house, and we set out. Two of the soldiers walked behind us, steering us to the wharf where we would embark for the Tower. Jacob came with us. He carried my bags, leaving me to walk freely and to look around the streets that I loved, now beginning to show signs of life in the fresh early-morning air. I felt panicked, my heart beating almost too fast to be held in my chest, and I kept drawing deep breaths and then forgetting to breathe between them. By the time we reached the boat I was lightheaded, nearly fainting, and when Jacob put his arm about my shoulders, I did not resist.

"Nell, if you are allowed, send letters. I need to know you are safe and well." Papa's voice was low and calm, but the pulse that beat in his forehead matched the throb of my own heart. I pulled away from Jacob and flung myself at Papa, desperate for the feel of his strong arms that had always kept me from harm. Now I was going where his protection would not reach. I longed to turn and run back to the house I had lived in all my life. But I felt, beneath the cloth of my bodice, the cold metal of Ned's ring, and I hardened my resolve. This was what I wanted, though not the way I'd wanted it to happen. I let Papa go, and he handed me a small leather purse. I looked inside; there was a pile of copper coins.

"Use it for food, for bribes—anything that will help you and your brother and the princes," he said.

"I will. And I will take care," I promised Papa, slipping the purse into my skirt pocket and taking Toby's hand. In my words were the promise to take care of myself, of Toby, of Ned and Dickon. The weight of all that obligation bowed my shoulders, but I straightened them with an effort and stepped into the boat, avoiding the hand one of the soldiers offered and helping Toby to jump in after me.

As the mists rose from the Thames and the damp spread beneath my cloak, our hooded boatman pushed off from the wharf and we moved into the current, pulling away from the bank. On the shore, Papa and Jacob stood motionless and straight, and we watched in equal stillness until their forms merged with the other shapes on the wharf and the distance hid them from our sight.

CHAPTER TEN

"Will we go in by Traitor's Gate?"

Toby whispered this to me as our boat approached the high walls surrounding the Tower. Though we'd never been inside those walls, everyone knew Traitor's Gate. Those who entered that way never came out again.

"Oh, I don't think so," I assured him, sounding more certain than I felt. He was shivering from the damp on the water, and I chafed his arms to warm him as we passed from early-morning sunlight into the shadow of the Tower.

We did not enter through the Gate but stopped at a waterside staircase and disembarked there, where a guard challenged us and then let us through a foot gate in the great wall. I could feel his eyes on us as we passed, and heard him say to his companion, "More babes for the Tower! They'll be hiring nurses soon!" The two soldiers snickered.

Inside, I was amazed to see that the Tower complex was not so grim as I'd imagined. Broad green lawns stretched between the ancient buildings. A family of ducks waddled down a cobbled path, heading past us toward the river. Groups of soldiers practiced their drills, while others sat under trees, obviously off duty. It seemed an oddly peaceful place, and I had to remind myself that here King Henry had died, and the Duke of Clarence, and Lord Hastings, and many, many others.

In the center of the whole complex was a square, squat keep of pale stone, as high as the outer walls, surrounded by a grassy border. The guard led us there, and he told us that this was the White Tower, where the prince and the king were living.

At the entrance, we were handed over to another guard. He ordered two soldiers to take our baggage, and we climbed a winding stair marked at spaces with window slits that let in very little light. The stair was broad but steep—Toby nearly had to jump from one step to the next. We were panting when we reached the top. The soldiers handed us our bags and pointed the way.

We proceeded down a short corridor and then turned into a large room. I was surprised at how grand it was: rugs covered the floor, tapestries lined the walls, the furnishings were of dark carved oak, and a blazing fire warmed the air. The windows looked out on the Thames far below, where ships moved upstream and downstream like toy boats on a trickling brook.

And there were the king and the prince, our Ned and Dickon, squinting at a chessboard. They looked up as we entered.

There was a moment of stupefied silence, and I realized that they had no idea we were coming.

Their uncle Richard controls what they know.

In the next instant, the chessboard was overturned, a cry went up, and Toby and I found ourselves hugged, pummeled, and very nearly squeezed to breathlessness.

"*Nell!*" cried Ned. "What are you doing here? How have you come? How long may you stay? Oh Nell, it is so good to see you!"

The words rushed out of him, tripping over one another, and I laughed through tears to see his happiness. He looked worn and pale, but his eyes were as clear as ever, and they sparkled with pleasure as he looked me over with such attention that I blushed.

"You've grown up a bit, Nell," he said.

My tongue became thick in my mouth and I could think of no tart reply. Instead, I stared at the floor, as speechless as any country maid. Ned laughed at my confusion, and a momentary annoyance freed my tongue. "I'm taller than you, at least! Is it right for a king to be shorter than the least of his subjects?"

But it was a lie; Ned had grown as well, and filled out, his shoulders broader.

"Tell me," he said, drawing me to a chair by the window as Dickon pulled Toby out of the room to show him the rest of their tower chambers. "How did you come here? And why? Was it because of the ring I sent?"

I lowered my voice. "Is it safe to talk here? Can any hear us?"

Ned shook his head. "I don't know how they could. The walls and doors are thick. Speak soft, and tell me the news."

I held out my moonstone ring. "When I received this, I wanted to come at once, but there was no way I could see to do it."

"I was in despair when I sent you that," Ned said, shaking his head regretfully. "I was not even sure that it would ever get to you; I slipped it to one of the soldiers who serves us, but I thought perhaps he would pocket it and give it to his sweetheart."

I pressed the ring into his hand. "Take it back. I'm here now."

Then I described the queen's plea, keeping my voice low. I didn't tell him that his mother had sent soldiers to take us. I thought that might be too much of a burden for him. "So you see, the ring gave me the conviction to come, but your mother gave me the means."

He sighed wearily. "It was wrong of her to ask. She has put you in peril."

"She is so alone. . . ." I wasn't sure what to say to Ned about the queen. My own feelings were utterly confused. She had been our benefactor, our protector, but in the end she had betrayed my father. I saw now that it was true what people said about her: she was a woman of great contradictions. Papa had been blind to them. We all had.

Ned stood and looked through the window, watching the river traffic below. "Have all her attendants gone?"

"All," I replied. "Even Master Thaddeus has been sent away, for safety's sake." I worried that this news would alarm Ned, so I added, "But she remains steadfast, as always. She is not afraid." And then I bowed my head, so he would not see the lie in my eyes.

He turned and forced a smile. "Nor am I, with you here. The days were long in this place when I was by myself, but now, with Dickon, and you, and Toby—oh, God forgive me, I am so glad you are here!" He clasped my hand tightly.

"Show me the Tower," I commanded him, springing up and freeing my hand. "Here I pictured you in a dank, dripping dungeon, but you're living in luxury! Is this what all prisons are like?"

Ned laughed. "Even the rest of the Tower is not much like this. These are the royal apartments—where my parents stayed before Father's coronation, as kings have done for a hundred years. But there are less-fine accommodations, and there are dungeons enough to hold half of Westminster. Come, I'll show you!"

We gathered up Toby and Dickon and went exploring. Ned and Dickon seemed to have the freedom of the place. We wandered unchallenged through the White Tower, admiring the Presence Chamber, where kings held court while at the Tower, and the Council Chamber, and St. John's Chapel, with its beautiful stained-glass windows.

Outside, we walked past the soldiers marching and practicing with their arms on the green. We paused at a small tower that bordered a beautiful garden, all abloom with flowers, and Ned said somberly, "This is the Garden Tower. This is where my uncle George died." We bowed our heads, and I said a silent prayer for the repose of the Duke of Clarence's soul—and tried not to think about the rumors surrounding his death.

When we started toward the Lion Tower, a guard intercepted us. He bowed and said, "Your Majesty, I must go with you." Ned nodded, and we walked in the soldier's company to the most wonderful part of the Tower of London, the menagerie.

"It was begun almost four hundred years ago," Ned told us as we gazed in astonishment at cages holding leopards, a lion, a camel, and a bear. "The leopards are the descendants of some sent to Henry the Third by the Holy Roman emperor. There were three then, for the three leopards on the Plantagenet arms." There were only two now, but one looked round and bulging, about to give birth. Their sleek, spotted coats rippled in the sunshine, and when the female yawned, we drew back at the sight of her long, sharp teeth.

"Would she eat a person?" Toby wanted to know. We turned inquiringly to the guard, and he nodded.

"Aye, and she has. Three years ago, a watchman was drinking on duty, and he slipped and fell into her pen. Torn to shreds, he was, by the time he was missed at the watch call." The guard made the sign of the cross to ward off evil, and we all did the same, staring at the delicate-looking beast.

"The bear, now," the guard went on. "He's a regular baby. See his links?" Around the bear's neck was a metal chain, which looked to be many yards long. "That's so he can reach the Thames water through the gate, to fish for his supper. You come some evening, and you can watch him fishing."

Toby was thrilled. Master Caxton had given him a bestiary on his name day a year before, and he'd spent many hours looking at the strange, wondrous beasts painted on its pages. To be able to see them alive, pacing or napping or grooming themselves, was more than he had ever dreamed of.

We watched the animals for a long time. I was especially

amused by the camel's ridiculous hump and long, mournful face. Every now and then it would spit with a noise that made me snort with laughter. Even Ned laughed to hear it.

Finally, as dusk fell, we started back to the White Tower. As we recrossed the moat we saw a procession of soldiers moving from gate to gate.

"What are they doing?" Toby asked.

"It is the Ceremony of the Keys," Ned told him. "See the man in the longest red coat?" Toby nodded. "He is the chief warder. Watch—he will lock all of the gates around the outer wall."

We watched as the chief warder walked with four soldiers—and another man whom Ned called the watchman—around the complex, locking each gate as he passed. Then, when they reached the Garden Tower, the tower sentry called out to them, "Halt, who goes there?"

"The keys," the warder replied.

"Whose keys?"

"King Edward's keys."

The sentry saluted. "Advance, King Edward's keys. All is well."

King Edward's keys. That seemed a good sign to me. Although the soldiers did not treat Ned as king, their ceremony still acknowledged him as ruler. I looked at Ned to see if he had noticed, and he smiled ruefully at me.

"My keys," he said, "but I cannot use them to leave."

We returned to the White Tower, and I saw what I hadn't

truly seen before: that guards were everywhere, at the entrance to each stair, in position in each corridor. Every footstep we took was watched, and, I had no doubt, reported to Richard of Gloucester.

Later, for dinner, we dined on tough mutton and cider, and I noticed that Ned hardly touched his meat. "Aren't you hungry?" I asked him, concerned.

"It's my tooth," he said. "It's been hurting me for weeks, and it's much worse when I take food." He touched his cheek and winced.

"I'll get you a cool cloth," I said, and called a guard to fetch a wet length of linen. I wound it around his head and over his cheek, and he seemed at once to feel better. "Tomorrow we'll send for a poultice, and if that doesn't work, we'll get a barber to pull it."

Ned shook his head. "No barber."

"But Ned, why? I've seen these toothaches before. They don't usually get better on their own."

"I daren't," he said miserably. "If I show any sign of weakness to my uncle Richard . . . who knows what he will do with it?"

I dropped the subject, though I planned to summon a barber on my own if the poultice didn't take. Still, for now his pain seemed eased, and while Dickon and Toby drowsed by the fire, Ned and I read aloud to each other from a copy of Aesop's *Fables* that I had tossed into my satchel when I packed.

But my long, sleepless night caught up with me, and finally my head drooped over the book. "To bed, Nell!" Ned said, making me jump.

I roused Toby, and Ned led us down the hallway to a comfortable chamber with one large bed and one small. We tucked Toby into the smaller, and Ned bade me goodnight.

"I am so happy you are here!" he said. "I know it's selfish of me, to be happy when you are in danger. I'm sorry, Nell. I can't help but be pleased when I see you."

I smiled at him and replied, simply, "I'm glad too."

· ● ·

I slept deeply, and when I woke I was alone, the room flooded with gray morning light. Toby was already gone, so I leapt up, feeling strong and rested and ready to face whatever the day had to offer.

After splashing my face in a silver bowl someone had filled with fresh water, I dressed and wandered down the corridor to the large room we had used the night before. The remains of a meal were scattered on the table, and I wondered whether there were servants here and when I would see them.

I took a crust of bread and a swallow of cider and looked out the window to the Thames below. A mist hovered over the water, and the sun struggled to shine, but I could see far from this room at the top of the tower: upstream and down; across the river to the wharves; farther still, to the woods and low hills beyond the city. It struck me that when Ned looked out, he looked upon the land that should, by all rights, be his. What torment it must be for him, trapped in this tower, knowing he was king of all he could see, and far more as well!

"Nell, you're up!" Toby came running into the room,

startling me. "We're going to shoot on the green. The soldiers have set up a target for us. Do come!"

I followed him down the steep stairs and out into the damp air. Ned and Dickon were already shooting at the target, and I marveled to see Ned's skill with the bow. He hit the center easily.

"Here, Nell, you shoot," he said when he saw me. At first I didn't want to. It brought back too clearly the memory of Lord Hastings, my old instructor, and the knowledge of his terrible death. But I didn't want to explain my reluctance, so when Ned handed me his bow, I took it. I hadn't shot a bow for years, and I was clumsy holding it.

"Give her mine," Dickon insisted. "That one is too big! Here, Nell, try mine!"

The smaller bow was more manageable, and when I held it, drew back the string, keeping the arrow steady, and let fly, I thrilled to the feel of it. My arrow soared straight a short distance, then wobbled and plunged to the earth. The soldiers standing about laughed, but a look from Ned silenced them. I was pleased to see the respect they granted him, and that they addressed him as "Your Majesty," not just "my lord."

We shot until my arm trembled and I could hold the bow no longer. By this time my arrows made their way to the target more often than not, though my shots were so weak that they bounced off rather than sticking. Toby fared much better, hitting the target's center more than once. I roughed up his hair as we left the green and told him I was proud, and he blushed, looking very pleased.

We passed several days peaceably like this, shooting in the morning, visiting the menagerie, playing chess and reading when it rained and in the evening. Ned's tooth seemed to improve with a poultice one of the soldiers brought after I slipped him a few coins. As we wandered through the Tower we met the resident ravens, huge black birds that I hated at once. Their hoarse voices made me shudder, and whenever I had to climb the stair they lived under, I clasped my skirts tightly to myself and ran past where I knew they sat, their beady eyes watching everything.

We also got to know the servants assigned to the king and prince, two men whom I liked no better than the ravens. One was Will Slaughter, a weaselly fellow with long, greasy hair, a pockmarked face, and a humble manner that belied the flash of his eyes. The other was a man from York named Miles Forrest, burly and red-haired, whose gaze rested often on me in a way that made me uneasy. They were likely supposed to be with us at all times, but they were lazy, and Forrest, at least, was not very bright. They attended the boys haphazardly, and Ned and I found ourselves doing much of the cleaning up and planning that kept our days running smoothly. I didn't object to these tasks, as the more time we spent on them the less we had to see of Forrest and Slaughter. We dared not speak much when they were with us, for it was likely that any word passing our lips would be repeated to Gloucester that same day.

I wrote in my book of secrets constantly, recording our activities and the princes' health. I thought that perhaps later, when Ned was released, the information might be useful.

Dickon teased the leopards today with a piece of bacon, and nearly lost a finger. Ned reprimanded him for being a fool, and he stamped his foot and then cried, saying Ned was not his father and couldn't tell him what to do. Then both of them felt terrible, and there were apologies all around.

· ● ·

Ned's tooth was much better today—until he bit into a meat pie and hit a piece of bone. Back to the poultice!

· ● ·

Toby told me he was angry at the queen for upsetting Papa. I made him understand that he mustn't let Dickon or Ned know what happened. It's best for them to think we came of our own choice. He worries about Papa, though, alone and himself worried about us.

· ● ·

This evening I looked at Ned as he was reading and thought, What if he were just an ordinary boy—a merchant's son, or a scholar's? In here, away from everything and everyone, it's harder to tell myself that such thoughts are wrong, or impossible.

One afternoon while I was reading aloud from *The Historye of Reynart the Foxe*, a heavy step sounded on the stair.

I stopped, and we all turned toward the doorway. Forrest came in, and behind him I saw Jacob's broad shoulders and familiar face.

I leapt up in surprise and ran to him, gladder than I could say to see him.

"Jacob!" Toby cried. "How is our father? How goes Master Caxton and the world outside?"

Jacob did not answer him but turned to Ned and knelt, laying the books he carried on the floor. "Y-Your Majesty," he said, stammering a bit.

"Ned, this is Jacob Langland, who works with Master Caxton. I have told you about him in our letters—you remember, don't you?" I was embarrassed, though I could not say why, and felt I was talking too fast.

"Please, rise," Ned said. "Welcome to our—to our prison. What have you brought us?"

Jacob stood, lifting the pile of books easily. "*The Game and Playe of the Chesse,* and *The Golden Legend,* Your Majesty. And a book of sermons in Latin. You see, this one has woodcuts. Master Caxton is especially proud of it."

Ned drew closer to look at the volumes. His love for books rivaled even Master Caxton's, though they loved them for different reasons. Master Caxton saw a book as a collection of pages, a challenge to be measured and cut and printed. For Ned, a book was a collection of ideas in words, a challenge to be explored and savored.

Jacob and the king thumbed through the books, and Forrest, growing bored, wandered from the room. As soon as he was safely out of earshot, Jacob motioned me over to the table. He spoke quickly, in a low voice.

"Your Majesty, Master Caxton, Master Gould, and your mother the queen have devised a way to communicate secretly, if it should be necessary. You see here—they have placed a tiny mark above some words in one of the books. The marks are only visible if you look very hard. They felt that the Tower guards would not think to search the books, and it seems they were right." He paused, and I stared at him, confused.

"Then," he continued, "if you string together the marked words, you will have a message. In the same way, when I take back the books from the previous week, you may mark words to send a message to Master Gould or to Her Majesty the queen."

The scheme seemed dangerous, even foolhardy, to me. "But we could simply send letters! Surely the king is allowed to write his mother!"

"But my words are read by many when they are sent by letter," Ned mused. "It is an interesting idea."

Jacob nodded. "Your mother the queen felt that if there were something secret you needed to tell, or if you learned or feared that Gloucester was ready to . . . to move against you, then she would need some way to know."

I shivered. We would be spies. If we were caught . . . Would it be treason? Would we be beheaded, like so many who'd gone to the Tower before us?

But Ned was pleased by the idea. "It will be like a game, Nell," he assured me. I looked at Jacob to see what he thought, but he would not meet my eyes.

"And what word from outside?" Ned asked. "What is happening? We know nothing in here!"

Jacob said, "Your Majesty, my lord Gloucester tries to

discredit you. This Sunday past—what should have been your coronation day!—he had the lord mayor declare that you are a bastard. He claims that King Edward was engaged to another woman when he married your mother the queen! He claims their marriage was not valid!"

Ned snorted so loudly that Forrest poked his head back in, and again we bent over the books. When he had gone, Ned said, "How can Uncle Richard say that? He knows it isn't true. Surely he goes too far!"

"No one seems to take it seriously," Jacob assured him. "The people are all for you, Your Majesty."

"And my lady mother?" Ned asked. "How is she?"

"I have seen her just an hour ago. She smiled at me, and said to tell you that all would be well. There is a letter from her, but your . . . attendant has taken it. I suppose he will give it to you after he has read it himself, to be sure it contains no treason."

Ned smiled. "She must be hatching a plan, my mother," he remarked, very quietly.

I was doubtful. What plan could there be to get him out of the Tower? No one escaped from the Tower.

Forrest came back in, holding the queen's letter. "Ye must go now," he said shortly to Jacob, and Jacob bowed again to Ned and gave Toby and me quick hugs.

"Tell Papa we are well!" I urged him. "And how is he?"

"Worried, but well," Jacob reassured me as he started out, nudged forward by Forrest. "I'll tell him you lodge in luxury and dine on meat and wine!" And with that, he was gone.

Ned's face was thoughtful. "Toby, Dickon," he said. "Go down to the Council Chamber, and take this Latin text with you. I want you to copy out the first two pages." The boys protested, but Ned was insistent. "You mustn't neglect your studies while we are here. Do as I say!" They gathered up the book and scurried out.

Ned turned to me as soon as they had left. "That man—that Jacob Langland. He looks at you, you know."

I was silent.

"He would make a good husband. He has a fine job. He seems kind."

Shocked, I looked up. "Ned—Your Majesty," I said. "Jacob and I have worked together in the printing shop for years. We're good friends. I have never encouraged him in any way. Yes, I know he—he is fond of me. But I am too young to think of marriage. And I would not marry Jacob."

Ned ran his hands through his curls till they stood on end, and then flung himself into a chair. "You must marry sometime," he said. "And twelve is not too young to begin thinking on it." It was true; Joan, the baker's daughter who had once tormented me in King Street, was already betrothed to Nick, now an apprentice in his father's candle shop.

"I have no interest in marriage," I insisted. "You cannot ask me to marry someone I don't love!"

"I have no right to ask anything of you at all," Ned said in a low voice.

I went and sat beside him. "You don't need to ask," I said clearly, and for once I didn't blush. "I will not marry Jacob, nor any other."

Ned drew in his breath sharply. "No, Nell, don't say that. You don't realize what that means. You and I can't wed, you know that, even when we are older. I can offer you nothing—nothing more than my father offered Jane Shore."

I looked away when he said that.

"And I would not do that to you."

I turned back and met his gaze steadily. No, he was not like his father. He would not marry for love and then break his wife's heart with dozens of other women.

"I wouldn't want you to do that," I whispered. "But my heart is yours, Ned, and it always has been. It always will be."

When I said that, his breath caught in his throat. He stood, and I stood too, and we gazed at each other. Then slowly I raised my head, and he kissed me.

That kiss changed everything for me. If I hadn't known it before, I knew at that moment that I loved Edward the Fifth of England utterly.

We pulled back from each other, gasping from the shock of our kiss, and I felt a blush rise red from my chest over my face. Ned, too, was flushed. We stared at the ground, for once speechless. Then, still not speaking, he sat again in the chair and pulled me down next to him. Silently we rested, arms around each other, feeling our pulses beat together. His warm breath stirred my hair, and my heart was full. We stayed like that for a time.

For this moment I was glad, and always will be.

CHAPTER ELEVEN

That evening we pored over the books Jacob had brought, searching out the marked words. As our list of words became sentences, I began to see that Ned was right; the queen did indeed have a plan. A soldier within the Tower, loyal to Ned and his mother, was to set a fire—a big fire—in the Tower's church, St. Peter's. As it flamed, and soldiers ran to fight it, we would rush to the Postern Gate and there be escorted to safety by other conspirators. We were to wait for a signal—four blasts from a horn—and then we would know it was time to flee.

"This is madness!" I whispered when we'd figured out the scheme. "How can it ever work?" But the boys were thrilled by the idea. At last, a chance for action! For a day and a night we waited anxiously, ready to flee at a moment's notice.

And then something happened to make us forget the escape.

Will Slaughter, whom we had all quickly learned to despise for his rough manners and easy cruelty, came to us in the evening as Ned and I played a fierce game of chess, cheered on by the younger boys. I was dismayed to see him, as he rarely approached us after sundown. The sly look on his surly face made me anxious, and he hung about in the doorway for some minutes before speaking.

"Well, my lord, you are rid of an uncle," he said at last, and spat into the corner. Ned froze, his hand on a pawn.

"What do you mean?" he demanded hoarsely. Our eyes met, and I could see the same hope in his that I felt: was it possible that the Duke of Gloucester had died?

"Oh, not His Grace Richard of Gloucester," Slaughter assured him, and barked a laugh. "Nay, it is your uncle Rivers who now lacks a head. My sympathies to ye, my lord!"

I crossed myself and whispered a prayer for Lord Rivers, whom we had mocked for his hair shirt and who had tried his best to teach Ned and keep him safe. Ned's chin quivered, but his voice was calm as he said, "Why do you address me as 'my lord,' Slaughter, and not 'Your Majesty'?"

"Oh, ye have not heard!" Slaughter crowed, delighted. "Today the council presented evidence that your father Edward was betrothed to another woman when he married your mother. His marriage to the queen, then, is null and void. Ye boys, and your sisters, ye're all bastards! Bastards, and not in line for the throne. The council has proclaimed your uncle king. He is Richard the Third of England, and he is to be crowned in a week's time."

Pleased, Slaughter leaned against the door frame to watch our reaction, and we struggled not to give him the pleasure. The little boys sat stock still; I gazed, trembling, at the floor; and Ned clenched his hands into fists. Finally he looked up at Slaughter.

"Thank you, Slaughter," he said tightly. "You may leave us."

Slaughter laughed, and spat again. "Ye should not be so high and mighty. Ye are not king, and shall never be! Sleep well, all ye babes, ye bastards and foundlings. Sleep well!"

He left us, and we sat in shocked silence. I dared a look at Ned and saw his face contorted, sorrow and shame and stark terror moving across it like dark clouds across the sky.

I went to him and took his hands. Then he wept, his tears setting off tears in Dickon and then in Toby, who could never bear to see anyone cry.

After a time, we dried our eyes. No one could think of anything to say, until Ned at last murmured, "We are done for."

Dickon gasped, and I moved to him and put an arm around his narrow shoulders. Then I spoke firmly. "Ned, stop. Gloucester has taken the crown, but he will not—he *dare* not do you harm. You heard Jacob; the people are for *you*. Such an act would cause a rebellion, and his claim is too shaky to risk it." I glanced at Dickon, hoping Ned would read in my look a warning to speak less gloomily in front of his little brother.

My words sounded reasonable, I knew, but my heart feared they were false. How could Richard keep the boys alive? If Ned's supporters knew he lived, the threat of an uprising in his name would never fade.

As Richard had killed King Henry to make sure King Edward's crown would never be challenged, so he would have to do the same to Ned and Dickon—his own nephews!—to ensure his claim to the throne. I could see this knowledge in Ned's eyes; all the hope had gone from them.

"We should go to the chapel and pray for your uncle Rivers," I said to Dickon, wiping his face and smoothing back his tangled hair. "He is at peace now. He is with God."

Far into the night we knelt in the damp chapel, but while the others prayed I thought feverishly, trying to figure out a way to help the princes. By the time the moon had set, I was exhausted and no closer to a solution.

We were utterly powerless, trapped in the kingdom's best-guarded prison, surrounded by hundreds of soldiers and walls thick enough to withstand any attack. Our only hope was the queen's plan: fire and confusion and escape. If that didn't succeed, we would have to resign ourselves to meeting our fate.

I tried to imagine what might happen. Would Richard have the princes beheaded? Hanged as traitors? Drawn and quartered?

And what of Toby and me?

By morning, Ned's mouth was inflamed again, made worse by a night on the cold stones of the chapel floor. I soothed him as best I could with cool cloths, but he groaned with pain and his eyes watered above his swollen cheek. I called for a poultice, but no one came, and no food or drink was brought to us all day. The guards would not let us leave the White Tower anymore.

Dickon and Toby are hungry, but they do not complain. They are quiet and don't even play. I try to make them smile with Master Thaddeus's silly riddles. Their lips turn up but their eyes are dull.

We are all so afraid.

In the middle of the night, we were awakened by a horn sounding.

I heard it blast once, twice, thrice, four times, and suddenly remembered Queen Elizabeth's wild plan. *It was the signal!*

Heart racing, I rushed to the princes' room. It had a window that faced the church, where the fire was to be set.

I could see nothing at first. Then a group of soldiers, one carrying a brand, came from behind the building. In the torchlight, I could see they held a man who kicked and struggled in their grasp.

I knew it was the soldier who was supposed to have set the fire that would free us.

"What has happened?" Ned asked from behind me. I shook my head, sure that if I spoke my voice would crack and I would dissolve in sobs. "They caught him? Nell, did they catch him? Is it over?"

"Yes," I whispered finally. "They have him. It is over."

Ned put his arms around me, and I could feel his heart beating through his nightshirt. His swollen cheek felt hot against mine. "I am sorry, Nell," he said, low. "I would not have had you hurt for anything. I wish there were some way . . ."

"I'm glad to be here," I told him, but I wasn't sure that I meant it anymore. I was afraid to die. I was afraid it would hurt, and I was afraid of what came after. Would I go to heaven? I tried to catalogue my sins, to see if their weight was enough to bear me down to hell, and I thought that maybe my greatest sin was that I wished I were free, away from the Tower and from Ned and from fear of death, safe in my bed in my papa's house.

Suddenly I thought of my mother. I could not remember her face or what she smelled like, but I remembered how it felt when she held me. I was tired, tired of being the one who comforted, the one who was responsible. I wanted someone to comfort me. I wanted my mother's arms around me, protecting me. I wanted my mother.

I pulled away from Ned, ashamed. "Try to sleep," I said, turning so he couldn't see the dread in my face. "In the morning I'll see if I can go to the garden, and maybe I can find some herbs to make a poultice for your tooth." I didn't wait for him to reply but fled the room, back to my own chamber, where I curled up with Toby in his little bed and lay, dry-eyed and sleepless, until dawn.

· ● ·

I barely remember the next few days. We were all heartsore and bewildered. When Jacob appeared with an armful of books in our parlor doorway, it took me several moments to figure out why he had come. It had been just a week since his first visit, but it seemed an eternity. In that week, Lord Rivers had lost his life, and Ned had lost his kingdom.

Neither Forrest nor Will Slaughter eavesdropped on us this time. Indeed, they seemed to have given up on us altogether.

It seemed absurd that Richard would allow Jacob to visit

us now. "I think he has forgotten about me," Jacob explained, drinking a goblet of musty wine we had found in a cupboard. "The guards seemed surprised to see me, but when I reminded them of my visit last week, they let me in."

When we asked what had happened with the queen's planned fire and escape, Jacob's mouth twisted. " 'Twas a foolish idea to start," he said, shaking his head. "There was only the merest chance that the man could start the fire without being seen, and he was half-drunk when he tried, poor sod. They took him before he laid flint to tinder. He was hanged on Tower Hill two days ago."

"What was his name?" Ned asked.

"Oh . . . Lovell, I believe. Yes, Thomas Lovell."

"I shall say a prayer for him," Ned said somberly. I reached out and touched his hand, and saw Jacob shoot a swift glance at me.

"And what of this claim that our father was engaged to another woman before he wed our mother?" Ned demanded. I could see that the question cost him in pride, but he had to know. "Where did such an idea even come from?"

"I'll tell you what I know," Jacob said. "I have the story from Master Caxton. The council was presented with a petition saying your father King Edward was betrothed to a Lady Eleanor Butler long ago. Years before he met your mother. He tired of Lady Eleanor and went on to marry your mother without breaking the contract. If he married when he was betrothed to someone else, the marriage was unlawful."

Ned's eyes were wide. "Is there evidence that my father was betrothed to this woman?"

"No one has seen any evidence that I know of, Your Majesty, but the council accepted it. That was when they proclaimed—well, they proclaimed that you and your brother were no longer in line for the throne. And that was when they offered the crown to Richard of Gloucester."

I tried to digest this story. Could it be true?

King Edward certainly had loved many women, as many before his marriage as after, or so rumor said. It seemed possible that he would have betrothed himself to one of them. But he was not a stupid man; he would never have married the queen without making sure the marriage was in every way lawful. He wouldn't have risked the future of the kingdom like that. No, I didn't believe it.

Not that it mattered, though. All the kingdom could disbelieve the story, but the council had accepted it. They had declared Ned and Dickon and the princesses to be bastards, and they had given the crown to Richard.

Ned sighed deeply. "We have written a letter to our lady mother," he said at last. "There is no message in the books for her. We saw no need for that. It is all ending, I fear, and I thought it best to . . . to say our good-byes. Will you be sure she gets it?" His tone was grave, and when I looked at him, his eyes seemed a century older than his years.

"I will guard it with my life, Your Majesty," Jacob promised, and he took the note Ned held out and slipped it into his shirt.

I could see he was alarmed, and he asked me to walk with him to the tower doorway.

"Nell, you must come away," Jacob said in a low voice, as soon as we were out of earshot. "I wish the king exaggerated, but he is right. And as he is in danger, *you* are in danger. I believe I can get you out. There are far fewer guards now. Come with me. Now's the time!"

I took a deep breath and shook my head. "Oh Jacob, look what happened to poor Lovell. They'd catch you, and you'd hang too—and so would I—if we tried such a thing."

"Nell, don't be foolish. You are no soldier; you don't need to die for your king! Let us *try*, at least."

Stubbornly, I stared at the floor, saying nothing. Jacob took my chin and tilted my head up, forcing me to look into his eyes. I pulled away, but too late. His steady brown gaze saw what I wouldn't say, and he scowled. Still, he tried once more: "What of your brother, Nell? What are you thinking? What can I tell your father?"

I flinched at his harsh words, thinking of Papa's fear for us, but I could not give in. I truly believed we would not succeed in escaping—and I could not turn my back on our friends. Not now.

"We will be fine, Jacob. I know we will," I said, as strongly as I could. And so I sent Jacob away with an aching heart, afraid that I wouldn't see him again, and more sorry for that than I could say.

· • ·

I stopped writing in my book of secrets. We ate little; the food, when we were brought any, was meager and nasty, and we had no appetite for it. Long hours were spent gazing out the window at the river below or watching the soldiers at their practice. At night sometimes I read aloud, but more often we lay before the fire staring at the flames, or slept uneasily for as many hours as we could force ourselves to. Ned's tooth tormented him, and Dickon developed a troubling cough and a nervous tic that caused his eye to squint. I made poultices as best I could, but I wasn't schooled in healing, and more often than not my concoctions peeled the skin off Ned's cheek or caused an itching rash on Dickon's neck.

We continued in this dull and dreading way for days; we had lost track of time. And then one night, when Toby and I were getting ready for bed, he said, "Nell, I don't understand something."

"What is it?"

"If Ned and Dickon are bastards now, and always were, as Gloucester says, then why should Gloucester be bothered with them? They could not be bastards and be king, could they?"

I stood still, my nightdress half over my head, trying to make sense of what Toby had just said. If the boys were illegitimate, then they could never be kings. If they could never be kings, then there was no reason for Gloucester to fear them. For just a moment I felt a flicker of hope. Of course. Of course! By making the boys illegitimate, Gloucester had removed the death sentence from them. They were no longer a threat to Gloucester's claim to the throne. They were no longer in danger!

And in the back of my mind, though I could barely admit it even to myself, this thought grew: if Ned were not king, if he were illegitimate, then he would not be so far above me in station. We would be more nearly equals. We might, someday, be able to marry.

Amidst those racing thoughts, though, doubt stood guard. It would be so much easier for Richard to rule without the princes, and so little trouble to do away with them. He was not a man to take chances. He lurked, and he planned, and he prevailed. That was the truth, and I knew it.

But I saw a way to climb out of our dreary hopelessness, at least, and I took it.

I pulled on my nightdress, ran to Toby, and grabbed him, thumping him about his head and shoulders. "I am such a fool!" I cried. "Of course you're right. Oh Toby, thank you!" My performance was good enough to convince him. We dashed down the hallway to the boys' chamber, where they lay awake after a day of dozing, and Toby announced his theory.

I saw a flash of life in Ned's eyes, but still he protested. "Uncle Richard will still want us gone. It will be simpler for him."

"No. As long as you are no threat—as long as you don't back an uprising or try to raise the people—he'll leave you alone. This way, he can show how gracious he is, how forgiving and generous."

"So we will live out our days—here?" Ned gestured around him. "I think death would be better."

Dickon whimpered, and I said, "Stop. You speak this way because your tooth aches so. You want your brother safe, don't you? And your uncle will let you out when all the excitement and talk has died down. I know he will!" I spoke very strongly, trying to persuade myself as well as Ned.

Ned smiled, wincing at the pain in his swollen cheek. "You do see the brighter side of things, Nell. But it makes some sense. You may be right. Oh, I do hope you are right!"

We talked far into the night, energized by hope, and finally fell asleep all atumble, wrapped in coverlets on Ned's broad bed. We slept till the late morning sun woke us, feeling rested and, for the first time in a long time, eager to face the day. But it was a day that brought only bad news.

After eating a large morning meal that we wheedled from the guard on the stairs, we heard a commotion down the hall and emerged from our parlor to see soldiers entering our bedrooms. Ned called to them to halt and explain their presence, and a lieutenant turned to him without saluting.

"My lord, we are packing your things. We must move you."

My mouth was suddenly too dry to speak.

"Where do you move us?" Ned demanded.

"To the Garden Tower, my lord."

"And why are you moving us?"

The lieutenant's assurance left him, and he would not meet

Ned's gaze. "King Richard has need of these apartments, my lord. He plans to lodge here before his coronation."

A strangled sound escaped Ned, and for a moment I feared he would run at the lieutenant in his rage. But he did not, and in a moment he was calm again. I thought of what a good king he would make, for his emotions didn't rule him as they had ruled his father. He was composed, thoughtful, intelligent. He could rule with reason, not with passion, and it seemed to me the country would be the better for it.

But instead, it was Richard who would be king, and what would he rule with? Cruelty, impulse, deception? What sort of kingdom would we live in if he reigned?

We had no choice. In short order our belongings were packed, and we were taken to the Garden Tower, the place where Ned's uncle George had died, hidden from sight of the White Tower so His Majesty King Richard the Third would not have to be reminded of our existence.

CHAPTER TWELVE

Our rooms in the Garden Tower were not nearly as nice as the royal chambers in the White Tower.

The Garden Tower was a defensive keep, and all the windows were mere slits, to shoot arrows through. The rooms were not as high up, so the damp rose to them, and they were not carpeted nor hung with tapestries. Even in the heat of July, the Garden Tower was cold and dank. It stank of mildew, and mold grew green in the corners. Mice and rats scrabbled in the walls, and I imagined that they came out after we snuffed our candles. I found it hard to sleep, picturing vermin climbing around on our things, maybe crossing the very beds where we lay.

We had only three chambers, one bedroom for Ned and Dickon, one for Toby and me, and one common room, where someone, we saw on the day we moved in, had set a table with food and drink. After the soldiers laid down our belongings, we gathered around the rickety table and had our meal in silence, uneasy with our new quarters and unwilling to talk about the future.

Ned finally broke the silence. "It is good this happens now," he said, shredding a heel of bread into tiny pieces.

"Why?" asked Dickon.

"The sooner he is crowned, the sooner we are safe," Ned explained. "Once the coronation is over, we can begin to hope for a return to calm and peace. And perhaps one day . . ."

I couldn't tell if Ned truly believed his own words, but they cheered the younger boys. We laughed and joked as we toured the tower from top to bottom, where a musty, dark staircase ended at an empty dungeon that made us all shiver with dread.

At the top of the tower, there was a trapdoor that led to a roof where we could peer between the crenelations to see the yard below. We spent hours watching the soldiers marching to and fro, even though we'd grown bored with them, and enjoying the sun and mist and fresh breezes on our faces. We could even see as far as the River Thames, to gaze at the barges floating past.

One morning we heard trumpet blasts, loud even through the thick walls of our tower, and we raced up the stairs and through the trapdoor to see what was happening. Below us marched scores of soldiers dressed in their finest, headed by lieutenants on horseback and trumpeters holding their golden instruments aloft, all heading to the Tower Green.

From our perch, we could see a long barge on the river decorated with flags bearing a wild boar, Richard of Gloucester's standard. The barge was curved at the bow; at the stern it had an enclosure of gilt-painted wood. In the weak sunlight it glittered like gold. I'd been on a barge like that once, on a pleasure cruise down the river with King Edward and Queen Elizabeth and their children. I wondered if it was the same boat, and I snuck a look at Ned to see if he recognized it. His face was expressionless.

Other boats floated nearby, filled with onlookers. As we watched, the barge docked at the Cradle Tower water gate. The rowers laid down their oars, and from the barge's enclosure emerged Richard, Duke of Gloucester, dressed in a purple mantle trimmed with ermine, and his wife, the Lady Anne, in cloth of gold. A cheer arose from the spectators on the river, and Anne smiled and waved, but Richard did not. His dark head was bare, his gait measured but slow. They came with their attendants through the gate and onto the Tower Green. A horse was brought for Richard, beautifully decorated, and he mounted without grace. I remembered what Ned had told me long ago about the pain he suffered, and I wondered if he felt it now. I hoped so. Lady Anne settled in a litter, and, accompanied by soldiers numbering in the hundreds, they passed through the land gate in the Byward Tower on their way to Westminster Abbey to be crowned.

Ned wept, angry tears coursing down his face. He was helpless to right this terrible wrong, and I grieved for him. But when the bells rang out, proclaiming the new king, he wiped his eyes and squared his shoulders, and we said nothing more about it.

It is done. Richard is king, the third of his name in England. I no longer love King Edward the Fifth. I simply love Ned.

· ● ·

Our lives settled into a routine. We rose, breakfasted on stale bread and sour cider—if available—and climbed to the top of the tower. If it didn't rain, we stayed there much of the day. If it was wet, we ran races on the stair or played chess in the common room, wrapped in cloaks against the damp. Another meal, usually tough mutton and cheese, was sometimes brought to us; we read or talked; when we began to yawn, we said our good-nights and went to sleep. There were no letters and no more visits from Jacob. Our isolation was complete.

I tried to keep our rooms neat and to keep myself and Toby clean, and I tended to poor Ned's incessant toothache and Dickon's cough, which did not grow worse but also did not abate. With the coppers Papa had given me, I tried to bribe the guards to bring us medicinal herbs, but they took my money and gave us nothing. Some nights, when Dickon kept Ned awake with his coughing, I sent Toby to their room and took Dickon into bed with me, where I could soothe him and cool his warm brow until he slept peacefully.

A fortnight or so after the coronation, we were visited by the new chief warder of the Tower, Sir Richard Brackenbury. Unlike the other men who had been assigned to guard us, Brackenbury was a gentleman, and he seemed kind. He had warm blue eyes and a reddish beard, and his attitude toward us was almost fatherly. He sent us better food and some rugs for the floor, for which we were immensely thankful. He stopped in to see us every few days and took a personal interest in Ned's and Dickon's health, bringing in draughts and poultices from his own physicians to aid in their recovery.

His presence was a comfort. He sat with us sometimes by the fire, playing games with the younger boys or reading aloud to them. Once, he said to Ned, "My lord, under my watch, I vow that no harm will come to you." His voice was sincere, and Ned was grateful.

He told us a bit of what had been happening outside the Tower walls.

"King Richard and Queen Anne are on their royal progress. They have been to Windsor and will visit many of their loyal followers to thank them for their support."

Ned snorted. "To bankrupt them, you mean! I'm sure that Uncle Richard will demand only the best of food and drink and entertainment, and his hosts will have to provide it."

Brackenbury smiled. "That may well be, my lord. At any rate, they will be back in Westminster in the fall, and then your uncle will take up the reins of state."

"And does anyone ask after me? My mother, her supporters?"

"Your mother is still in sanctuary. She is well, but she cannot leave, nor are any allowed to visit her. I write to her often, though, and tell her how you fare."

Ned sighed, resigned, and we waited and passed the days, hoping that the time would come when King Richard would see fit to release us from captivity.

As August passed, we heard from Brackenbury of the king's progress through Coventry, Leicester, and Nottingham, and then to York, the seat of his power. We heard that he made his son the Prince of Wales, once Ned's title. Ned said nothing at the news.

I thought often of Papa during this time, wondering how he was and worrying that he feared for us. I tried, through Brackenbury, to send a letter to him, but though Brackenbury was sympathetic, he told me that he was under strict orders to keep us from communication.

"I am sorry, my dear," he said, and I believed him, for his bright eyes were clouded. "I will try to send word to your father unofficially that you are well and in good spirits. I am a father myself, and I know he must be concerned for your well-being."

With September came a change in the air. The evenings were a little crisp, and the light had that peculiar clarity that only autumn brings, when colors are muted but pure, and the smell of apples and dry leaves lingers. We longed to be outside, able to run and stretch ourselves, but we had to be content with our platform in the sky.

One day we lay out in the sunshine, trying to banish the cough from Dickon's chest with the day's warmth, and talked of what we would do if we were freed.

"I would go back to Ludlow," Ned said dreamily, lying back on one of the cushions we had carried up the stair. "It is remote enough to be safe, and it has a certain wild beauty to it. If I hadn't been so lonely, I would have loved it there."

I was surprised. "Wasn't it dark and dreary?" I asked.

"No, not really. The castle seemed that way at first sight, but inside it was quite comfortable. We had cushions and rugs and hangings, and the fireplaces were large and hot. And the countryside! Wild birds and game everywhere, and hills covered with purple heather. I remember the call of rooks and the smell of wild thyme. . . ." He drifted off into a reverie, and I joined him in dreaming of Ludlow, a place that sounded like a haven of safety and freedom. A place where he and I could be together in a way that would be impossible anywhere else.

"What about us?" Toby asked, interrupting my thoughts. "Will we go, too?"

Ned smiled without opening his eyes. "Of course you will. You both, and Dickon. And your father. We will all be there, together."

"We'll have such fun," Toby murmured.

For a time we lay sprawled, soaking up the warmth; then I rose and looked lazily out over the Tower yard. Below, I could see Brackenbury talking with a man I didn't know. He was short, with a shock of greasy hair, and wore a black cloak; they were arguing, but hard as I strained, I couldn't make out their voices. Finally, Brackenbury handed something to the man and stormed off, and I watched the stranger walk to the foot of the Garden Tower, below us. He opened his hand, and with a feeling of alarm, I saw what Brackenbury had given him: keys.

The man used the keys to open the tower door, and I stepped back, suddenly faint. Was he coming up to find us? He had an unsavory look to him. I didn't want to frighten the others, not now, so I walked casually to the trapdoor and stood over it. With my skirts masking my movements, I used my foot to slide the bolt and lock the hatch. Now, even if the man were to try, he could not get to us.

I spent the next hour in a panic, waiting for a hammering at the trapdoor that never came, trying to hide my fear from the others. At last clouds moved in, covering the late afternoon sun, and with a sudden thunderclap, cold rain poured down on us. Stunned out of their drowsy state, Ned and Toby tried to raise the trapdoor, but the bolt, rusty from little use, had stuck.

"By the saints!" Ned swore, kicking at it. "Nell, why did you lock it?"

I joined him in pulling on the bolt. "I . . . I don't know. I thought I saw someone enter the tower. I was afraid."

"Someone came in? Who?"

I looked at him, rain plastering his golden curls to his cheeks. I didn't want him to lose the pleasant glow the day had given him, and so I lied. "It was just a servant, but by the time I realized, the bolt was already stuck."

"I'll pull, you push," Ned said, shaking his head at my foolishness. We tugged at the bolt, and finally it scraped open and we scrambled down the stair, soaked to the skin.

The soaking brought on Dickon's cough again, so that night I agreed to take him into my room, leaving Toby to sleep with Ned. Before we slept, I looked carefully through our rooms, but I could see no sign of disturbance. Perhaps it had been nothing.

I slept uneasily, awakened over and over by Dickon's hacking cough and by my own wild dreams. Once, I dreamed the leopards had escaped from the menagerie and were pacing down the hall outside my chamber, and I awoke in a sweat, my heart beating wildly. I lay still for a moment to catch my breath, and then I heard what I had heard in my dream: footsteps outside my door.

A man's boots, moving down the hall.

I lay as though paralyzed, listening as hard as I could, but the walls were thick. This had something to do with the man I'd seen earlier, I was sure. He had come inside and hidden and prepared . . . what?

The boots stopped outside Ned's room, and the door creaked open.

Then all was quiet. What was happening in there? My mind conjured up pictures that were horrifying beyond bearing. The booted man, plunging a knife into Ned's heart as he slept, then Toby's. Wrapping twine around their necks until the breath left them. Holding a pillow over their noses and mouths as they woke and thrashed in desperation.

I wanted to gather up Dickon and flee, but I knew I would get no farther than the outer door of the tower, so I lay motionless.

It seemed to me that I heard a moan, though it could have been my own voice escaping from me. I was as filled with dread as if I were still in my dream, but the pain I felt when I dug my nails into my hand told me that I was awake.

I could not say how long it was before I heard the footsteps move back down the hall again. I tensed, terrified that the man would come into my room. I was ready to protect Dickon if he did—to fight, if I really had to, with my teeth if nothing else.

But the steps did not hesitate at my door. An instant later I heard them on the stair, and then all was quiet—all but my heart, hammering in my chest so hard it shook my whole body.

CHAPTER THIRTEEN

I lay without moving. I *couldn't* move. I knew that something terrible had happened, but I didn't dare think on it.

I wanted desperately to run to Toby, to Ned, but I didn't have the courage. Instead, I forced myself to reach out, feeling for Dickon's warm hand, clutching it with my icy one. He turned and murmured, "What?"

"*Shh!*" I hissed. "*Don't make a sound!*"

As silently as I could, I rose from my bed and scrabbled in the darkness to find my clothes. I pulled them on over my nightdress. Then I got Dickon up and dressed him.

"Your lady mother bids us go," I whispered, hoping he wouldn't question a command he thought came from his mother. "But we must be very, very quiet."

We tiptoed to the door, and I pressed my ear against it, listening. All was still outside. I eased it open, wincing as the rusty hinges squeaked. We squeezed through into the pitch-dark hallway. I took one of Dickon's hands in mine, and with my other hand I felt along the rough wall, guiding us forward.

We came to Ned's chamber door, and I hesitated.

"Stay here," I whispered to Dickon, and he stopped obediently.

I lifted the latch and opened the door. All was darkness and silence within. I stood as still as I could, listening. There was no movement. There was no breath. There was no life in this room, not anymore.

Numb, I backed into the hallway, took Dickon's hand again, and started toward the stairs. Our breathing sounded loud in the unnatural silence. I prayed that Dickon wouldn't cough.

I had no idea what I was doing. When we reached the tower door, what would be waiting for us? Would it be closed, shutting us in like rabbits in a hutch? Would there be soldiers, ready to grab us and march us to our deaths? And if we were lucky enough to slip out—and to escape being seized—where would we go? I hadn't spent any time in London town, though it was close to Westminster. I didn't know my way around the maze of streets and alleys there. We would be hopelessly lost—and easily caught.

But we couldn't stay here. We couldn't.

We found the stairs and eased our way down blindly, feeling for each step with our feet. When we reached the bottom, I felt for the outer door and pushed it open. It was unlocked!

There was no moon, but the torches placed at intervals

along the outer Tower wall made it easy to see, after the darkness of the stairwell. I knew there were few guards stationed at night—for who could escape from the Tower? There was one at the main gate, and one at each Tower building, but there were other entrances that were left locked and unguarded. *Perhaps* . . .

I looked around for the soldier who usually guarded our tower. There was no sign of him. Had he been dismissed, then, so that . . . whatever happened within could take place?

I placed my finger over Dickon's lips to signal silence, and we began creeping along the tower wall. I tried to picture the layout of the Tower complex that I'd seen so often from the roof of the Garden Tower. We needed to find a gate that led outside the walls, but even then, it must be the right one. I was pretty sure that the Iron Gate would take us to the wharf. Most of the other gates exited to the moat.

Silently, we made our way to the edge of the Garden Tower. There was a stretch of open grass we would have to cross to reach the Lanthorn Tower, and then the Well Tower. The Iron Gate was in front of the Well Tower.

"Follow me," I whispered.

My head down, I gripped Dickon's hand and began walking across the lawn. There was no way to avoid it. We were as visible as if it were high noon.

We had almost reached the wall of the Lanthorn Tower when a shout rang out. I froze. My terror was absolute; I couldn't even imagine what Dickon was feeling.

In the flickering torchlight I saw a guard cross the green

in front of the White Tower. He met another guard there, and handed him a jug. They were drinking on duty! But they had only called out to each other; they hadn't seen us.

We waited until they disappeared into the shadows behind the White Tower, then continued our creeping pace. A growl came from the Lion Tower, where the leopards lived. They were often restless at night. Along the Lanthorn to the Well Tower. Around the Well Tower to the Iron Gate.

And, of course, it was locked.

Dickon turned his face up to mine. I was glad I couldn't see the expression in his eyes. Of course it was locked. I knew it would be locked. But I had no other plan. Perhaps, if we waited, someone would go in or out. Then we could sneak past to freedom. It was a stupid idea, but it was all I had.

Then, all at once, we heard the doors of the Iron Gate squeal as they opened.

My heart leapt in my chest. I pulled Dickon to me and tugged the hood of his cloak down low over his face. "*Not a word*," I warned.

Heavy footsteps came toward us, candlelight casting wild shadows on the stone wall at our backs. The light made me blink; I could barely see who held the candle. A man—tall and cloaked and bearded. And familiar.

I sagged against the wall. It was Brackenbury, holding a candle whose flame flickered in the breeze from the Thames.

"Thank God, Nell, " he said in a low voice. "I couldn't get in to you. I knew—How did you—No, never mind. You and your brother, come with me. Now!" He turned and started back through the gate. It took me a moment to realize what he'd said. *You and your brother . . .*

In the dim light I could see Dickon's eyes widen. "Brackenbury thinks you are Toby," I whispered to him. "We must keep him thinking that. Can you do it?"

Confused, Dickon nodded. He was a smart boy, but he was very frightened, and I didn't know how well he could keep up such a masquerade.

"Keep your face turned away. Stay in the dark. Don't catch anyone's eye. Let me talk; say nothing."

He nodded again.

We hurried through the gate behind Brackenbury and out into the night air. There were no soldiers in sight, but there would be soon enough. I knew that Brackenbury was risking his life to help us. We walked quickly, heads down, along the wharf.

"I must leave you here. I'm sorry. I have to think of my family. But I've sent word. Someone will come for you," Brackenbury said when we reached Tower Hill. He turned to leave us.

I could bear it no longer. "Wait!"

He turned back, and by the light of his candle I could see lines in his forehead where before there had been none. He would not meet my gaze.

"Please . . . tell me."

He shook his head, and I saw that tears stood in his eyes. "Go, my dear. Leave London; leave England altogether if you can. The line of King Edward the Fourth is no more."

Dickon slumped against me, and I caught him and held him upright with all my strength as Brackenbury disappeared down Iron Gate Street. *The line of King Edward the Fourth is no more.* We both knew what the words meant.

Prince Dickon and I were left in London town, alive and well, while Ned and my beloved brother Toby lay dead in the bedchamber of the Garden Tower.

We stood for a short time in the dark, damp London air, leaning against the wall of a house whose inhabitants slept inside, unknowing. *You must run*, I kept telling myself, but my legs wouldn't move, and I couldn't tell if Dickon had fainted or was only as weak-kneed as I. Suddenly, through the wet air, a voice hissed my name.

"Nell! Nell Gould! Where are you, Nell?"

I shrank back against the rough stones. My legs suddenly had strength again, and I vowed I would not escape death in the Tower only to find it outside the walls. I turned to flee, but a hand spun me around, and I found myself clasped to a wet cloak. The arms holding me were Jacob's.

"Nell, are you all right?" he asked urgently.

I could not reply, but nodded feebly.

"And Toby?"

I nodded again, swallowing tears.

"Then come! We must begone. The queen sent me here. One of Brackenbury's men got word to her, and she knows all. She has arranged for you to get away, to be safe. But we must hurry!"

With one strong arm around me and the other around

Dickon, he hurried us down the deserted street, our hoods pulled low. After some twists and turns through roadways I didn't know, Jacob brought us to a rundown tavern. The sign above the door, barely readable, named it the Golden Hart. No innkeeper greeted us as we entered; the downstairs room, vast and filled with wooden tables and benches, was completely empty.

We sat at a rough table, still silent, as Jacob built up the fire in the huge fireplace at the far end of the room. He brought us tankards of cider and a plate of bread, but we couldn't eat. As the warmth spread through the room and I sipped at the cider, I began to unclench myself, and in a moment I was shaking as badly as if I had the ague. The table trembled with me, catching Jacob's notice, and he sat down and pulled me to him until I gained control of myself again.

"Hush, Nell, hush," he murmured. "It's all over now. You are safe. You are safe." His gentle voice lulled me, and I nearly slept. On my other side, Dickon put his head on the table to doze, and as he did so, his hood slid back, showing his golden hair. I felt Jacob's sharp intake of breath.

"*That is the prince!*" he cried.

"Be quiet!" I commanded him, pulling away. I tugged Dickon's hood back over his hair.

Jacob looked down at me, utterly bewildered. "How is it . . . where is Toby? Why is Prince Dickon here?"

I looked at the table, tracing its surface with my fingers. Decades of drunken men, carving with their knives, had left bumps and grooves and obscene pictures on it, all coated with a sticky film of dried ale.

"Toby is dead," I said, my voice dull. "He died instead of Dickon. The prince was with me because he was ill. It was he who was meant to die." Then I looked swiftly to see if Dickon had heard me, but he was asleep.

"What shall we do?" Jacob whispered. "We have the prince, alive! Oh, how I wish Master Caxton were here! He would know what to do!"

His helplessness—and my own fear—made me angry, and anger made me cruel. "Don't be afraid," I said harshly. "There is nothing anyone can do now—certainly not you. It's out of our hands, isn't it?"

And indeed, at that moment, we heard horses come into the yard, and then the door flew open. At first I couldn't make out the figure in the dark doorway, but an instant later I was in Papa's arms, sobbing wildly, trying to find the safety I had known there as a child.

Papa soothed me. "We will take you and Toby to a secure place, and there we can stay until it's safer. Oh, my dear, I am so sorry!"

You and Toby. I could say nothing.

I stood silent, filled with dread as Papa moved to the side of the sleeping Dickon and bent to kiss him.

I saw his face register the knowledge that this was not his son. He was bewildered at first. I could tell how his mind was working: *Where is Toby? Why is Dickon here and not Toby? But*

Ned and Dickon were killed. Only if Dickon is here, it was not Dickon who died. . . .

It was agony to see in his eyes the dawning realization of what must have happened to the boy he loved best in the world.

Finally Papa spoke brokenly. "We must away. Quickly. Before they find out what has really happened. If the king knew that Dickon was alive . . ." He didn't need to finish.

"Jacob," Papa said then. "Go back to Westminster. Get to the queen. Tell her what has happened. Help her get her people to Gravesend. We will meet them there." Jacob nodded wordlessly. He looked at me for a long moment, then, still silent, turned and left the inn.

Papa had brought two horses, one for me and the prince, one for him. I woke Dickon enough to help him stagger out into the stableyard and mount. Then I climbed up behind him, holding him tightly around the waist. In the foggy gloom of predawn London we rode away, slowly so that we would not attract attention. Papa rode first, then Dickon and me behind.

There were no soldiers in the streets. It was clear that King Richard did not yet know that his plot had not entirely succeeded. That Prince Dickon had escaped.

We traveled on the smaller streets, up Seething Lane to Crutched Friars, and finally came to Aldgate, the city gate out of London. There, guards stood at their posts.

"Who goes there?" a soldier demanded, standing beside his long lance. I could barely make him out in the fog.

"A butcher and his family, going to Dagenham. My farm is there." My father's voice was calm and quiet.

"Ye're out early, Master Butcher."

"Yes, we plan to go and come back before sundown. It's a long way."

The guard stepped forward and peered at us. I made sure that Dickon's hood was pulled low over his sleeping face, and held my breath.

"Pass, then, Master Butcher," the guard said at last. I breathed again. The horses' hooves clopped against the ground as we slowly went through the gate, and then we were out of the city.

We sped up as soon as we were away from the gate, but we were careful. Whenever we heard a horseman or carriage approach, we left the road and stood silent behind a hedge or copse of trees. If they came upon us unexpectedly, we lowered our heads and tried to look like a family on an early-morning journey.

"Where are we really going?" I asked Papa when we were alone on the road.

"To Tilbury."

Tilbury was twenty miles or more. "But why?"

"We must get Dickon away," Papa said in a low voice. "It's his only chance."

"Away—where?"

"To France."

France! How could we send this ill, frightened little boy so far? I tightened my grip on Dickon.

The sun never managed to burn off the fog that day. It was chill and dark for September. We traveled through the dimness for hour after hour. My thoughts fell into the rhythm of the horses' clopping hooves, and circled round and round. *Toby is dead. Ned is dead. It is your fault. It is your fault. Toby is dead. Ned is dead. It is your fault. It is your fault.* I wondered if Papa blamed me, and then I wondered how he could not blame me. It was unbearable, yet I welcomed the pain. I deserved it.

Finally Dickon stirred in my arms and raised his head.

"Where . . . ?" he began, but his cough kept him from finishing.

"We're riding to the coast," I told him.

"I want Ned," he managed.

"Oh, Dickon," I said, holding him even more tightly. "So do I. So do I." I wondered how much he understood of what had happened. His next words dispelled my doubt.

"He is dead, isn't he? And Toby too?"

"Yes," I said simply.

I felt Dickon's hot tears dropping on my hands as they clutched his waist, but he didn't make a sound. After a time he stopped weeping, and we just rode, on and on.

· ● ·

As the day began to wane, I heard galloping hooves behind us, and I turned to Papa in panic.

"Into the wood!" he ordered, for we were beside a thick stand of trees. I urged my horse off the road quickly, and we stopped when we were well hidden. A group of soldiers thundered by, and Dickon trembled in my arms.

"Do they look for us?" I whispered to Papa.

"Maybe," he said, low. "The king would know by now what has happened."

He said no more, so as not to scare Dickon, but I understood that to let Dickon escape could cost King Richard his kingdom. He had committed regicide—the murder of a king—for Ned had truly been the king of England. For Ned's supporters, Dickon, next in line for the throne, was now the true king. King Richard must be desperate to find Dickon. To kill him as he'd killed Ned.

We stayed off the road after that, making our way to Tilbury through fields and marshes. Our horses were exhausted, and we were too. I fell asleep in the saddle, almost sliding off once, but Dickon pinched me awake. The sky was darkening, and the fog rolling in, when we at last reached the outskirts of Tilbury.

"Will they be guarding the gate?" I asked Papa.

"Probably," he said. "But we don't need to go in through the gate. We can circle around to the harbor. We will have to leave the horses here."

We stopped at a small farmhouse with a neat stable attached, and Papa knocked on the door. A woman answered, wiping damp hands on her apron, her face flushed from the cooking fire. There was a short discussion, capped by a gold coin that Papa handed her, and our horses were led to the stable by her son, a boy my age who gave us a curious look but said nothing.

"You ride on my shoulders now, child," Papa said to Dickon. It was clear he did not want to speak the prince's name.

He bent down and lifted Dickon high, and then we were off again, stumbling across fallow fields and sheep pastures. It seemed miles before we could smell the salty water at the mouth of the Thames, mixing with the ocean. I scrambled to keep up with Papa, with no breath left for questions.

The walls of Tilbury did not go all the way to the river, so it was easy for us to get to the water's edge. There was a wharf and a long pier that disappeared into the fog. Dozens of small boats were moored near it.

"There is no ship here big enough to get to France," I said to Papa.

"No," he replied. "The ships for France sail from Gravesend—across the river."

"But how will we get across?"

"There should be a ferry," he said. "I'd heard there was."

There were workers on the wharf near the pier, and Papa left me with Dickon while he went to confer with them. He was soon back, his face grim.

"The ferryman will not go in the fog. We shall have to row ourselves."

"Row!" I exclaimed. "In what?"

I had only ever been in a boat twice: once when King Edward and Queen Elizabeth took us on the pleasure cruise down the river, and once to go to the Tower. I couldn't swim a bit, and I feared the water; there were mud, and eels, and other nasty things in its brackish depths. I thought of the pike in the ponds at Westminster that had scared Princess Cecily so with their sharp teeth, and I shuddered.

"I've hired a boat," Papa explained. "We're to leave it at the quay in Gravesend."

We followed Papa down to the pier, where a stocky fellow stood holding a rope tied to a small wooden skiff. I stared across the water. There was nothing to see but fog. How would we ever find our way?

"How far is it, Papa?" I asked.

"Not far. Less than a mile."

Papa lowered himself into the boat first, and I handed Dickon down to him. At that moment we heard a shout, and I looked up to see soldiers racing across the docks, armor and swords clanking.

They were headed straight for us.

CHAPTER FOURTEEN

I leapt into the boat, rocking it wildly, and Papa yanked the rope from its owner's hand before the man realized that it was us the soldiers wanted.

"*You! You with the boat, you stop, hear!?*" one of the soldiers shouted.

Papa scrambled to the middle seat and took up the oars—and with one strong pull, our boat leapt away.

We skimmed through the water as the soldiers ran down the pier, above and nearly parallel with us. I feared that one would leap from the quay and land in our boat, but they knew that the weight of their armor would sink them. So when they reached the end of the pier they stood helpless and furious, shouting and threatening as we pulled away. In another minute we reached deep water, and the fog swallowed us up. The soldiers' voices echoed, but we couldn't make out their words.

In silence and nearly blind, Papa rowed. We couldn't tell if the soldiers were following us by boat, and we dared not make a sound.

There was only the noise of the water lapping against the skiff, the oars dipping, and the gulls shrieking above the fog, invisible. Dickon shivered beside me, and I held him tight to try to warm him.

Suddenly a huge shape appeared out of the mist—a barge, returning from London after leaving cargo at the docks there, no doubt. It was enormous compared to our little craft and could crush us without even realizing.

I screamed and clapped a hand over my mouth, and Papa strained at the oars so hard that the veins stood out on his forehead. The skiff angled sharply to the left, and the barge brushed us with its tall wooden sides, rocking us violently. Startled by my cry or the abrupt movement, Dickon was thrown into a paroxysm of coughing, and I pulled his face into my cloak, trying to muffle the sound.

The barge passed without any of the men on board noticing us at all. Papa stopped rowing for a moment to catch his breath, his face damp and red. Then he took up the oars again, carrying us forward with wide, labored strokes.

I watched the barge disappear into the fog and remembered a game we played during the long afternoons when we sat atop the Garden Tower. Barges came past the Tower of London almost constantly, bringing goods to the city, taking goods away. We would point them out and then guess what they carried. Wool, bound for the Continent? Cheeses from France? Grain for Londoners' bread and beer? It had been Toby's favorite pastime. Tears burned in my eyes at the memory, but I didn't let them fall.

At last we could see the shore on the other side. Papa directed the skiff so we would not come into the Gravesend wharf, for we feared that there would be soldiers waiting there as well. We pulled the craft up on the muddy riverbank far enough from the wharf that it could not be seen, and Papa looped its rope around a willow tree that overhung the water.

"I gave the man enough to pay for the entire boat," he said to my questioning look. "He can buy a new skiff if he doesn't find this one."

Dickon bent over double, coughing. It was hard to breathe in the thick fog, even for me. "Papa, we must get him warm and give him food," I said urgently. "He's not been well these last weeks. That's why . . . that's why he was with me last night, and Toby was not."

Papa's face twisted as he took in my words, but he looked at poor Dickon with concern. "We cannot, daughter. We must get him safely away. Food and rest will do him no good if it means the king's men catch up to us."

I saw the wisdom in that.

"This next part is yours, Nell, I'm afraid," Papa said. "The soldiers in Gravesend may know to look for a butcher, so I cannot go. They may know to look for a man and a boy and a girl together, so we cannot all go. But they don't know to look for a girl alone."

I took a deep breath. "Yes," I said. "I see. What should I do?"

"Make your way along the wharves. Go through the town and look for Jacob, or for any of Queen Elizabeth's men you recognize."

"I can do that." I hugged Dickon, whose fevered hands

clutched hotly at me, and kissed my father, and then I picked my way through the Gravesend marshes toward the docks.

There were soldiers everywhere, it seemed. I dodged from doorway to doorway, grateful now for the fog. One soldier stared at me, and I tried to shrink inside my cloak, tried to disappear. But he only tossed me a penny, shaking his head at my scruffy appearance. I was muddy and damp and looked like any other street urchin.

I wandered through streets and alleyways. Gravesend was bigger than I had thought. I peered into pub windows and shops and people's houses, but I saw no one I knew. I began to feel desperate. What would I do if I couldn't find Jacob? Surely the soldiers would get word of what had happened in Tilbury, would begin to search the riverbanks before long.

I passed an alleyway off the main street and saw three soldiers talking. One of them glanced at me, then away. Then he looked again. My heart leapt in my chest as he opened his mouth to call out something.

I wouldn't have thought that my legs could still move, I was so tired, but the rush of fear I felt as the soldier shouted pushed me forward. I darted around a corner, then down one alley and up another.

I saw a soldier turn the corner in front of me, and I spun to flee back the way I'd come. But behind me came two more armed men. I was trapped.

In a flash, I thought of Joan, the baker's daughter from King Street. I could almost hear her mocking laugh and the way her tone turned falsely meek when she spoke to gentlemen and ladies at her father's bakery. I reached into my pocket for the little leather purse Papa had given me when I went into the Tower. It held only a few coppers now, but the soldiers didn't know that. As the men approached, I held it up.

"Oh, good sirs, I din't mean to do wrong, I din't! I was just that hungry!" The voice I spoke with was Joan's. I had no idea where it had come from, but I kept on. "The lord will never even miss his purse. Don't take a girl whose stomach has been empty these past two days! Don't put me in jail! Don't let them brand me!" The soldiers stopped in confusion.

I tossed the purse up in the air, and when the soldier in front of me reached out instinctively to catch it, I ducked under his arm and sprinted away.

Even exhausted, I was much faster than men in armor could be. I lost them after the third turn—and lost myself as well. I was now deep in the bowels of Gravesend. I had no idea where the main street was, or the harbor. Or my father's boat.

Weary and frightened, I wandered, stopping at each corner to make sure no soldiers were searching for me. Darkness had fallen when a staggering sailor pushed open the door of one of the inns, and I heard a voice I thought was familiar. It was a man speaking, quick and high-pitched.

I had to think hard to place it. Then I was sure, or nearly so. I pulled open the door and ducked inside.

The room was warm—hot, in fact, with a fire blazing on the huge hearth and a crush of bodies at small wooden tables pressed close together. No one paid me any mind as I pushed past serving maids, workmen, soldiers, and women whose low-cut bodices and unbound hair signaled their profession.

I heard the voice again, unmistakable now, and I saw the speaker at a table with three other men—it was Master Thaddeus, the royal fool. He was dressed in ordinary clothes, but his slight size and leathery features were unmistakable. Though two of the others were unknown to me, the third was Jacob. I could hardly believe I'd found them.

I made my way over to the table and sat on the bench beside Master Thaddeus without speaking. And all four glanced at me and then away. Ale and cider came, and we drank, and after a time the fool leaned against me and put his lips to my ear.

"Have you a boat?" he asked low, smiling gaily as if he spoke of sport or love.

I nodded, forcing my own lips into a wide curve that I hoped looked like a smile.

"Row to the *Grace Dewe*. She's anchored off the Lower Wharf, but far enough so you cannot see her from shore. They'll be waiting for you."

"How will I know her?" My mouth ached from smiling so hard.

"She flies the French flag. She's bound for Calais. As am I."

I grasped his hand. So Master Thaddeus would tend to Dickon on the journey! Thank heaven the prince would travel with someone he knew.

"He's ill," I told the fool. I hoped he would know who I meant.

"So Jacob said. There's a physician on board."

I stood up. The fool motioned me to bend down again, and he said, "A riddle: It's in your hand though you cannot feel it; only you and time can reveal it. What is it?"

I shook my head.

"Fate, my dear. Fate," said Master Thaddeus. He put a warm hand over mine, and I felt a little strength come back to me. Then he said, "Here is another one. See if you can guess it." He lowered his voice to a near-whisper and said:

"The twin of a prince, but with no royal kin;

A witness to murder, though no blood was shed;

She once saved two kings, through both courage and fear,

And one still lives on, but the other is dead.

Who is she?"

I drew in a quick breath, and he smiled at me, though his green eyes were sad. "You've done well, child. God be with you."

Jacob glanced up at me, his face pale and drawn. I could read the question in his expression: *Are you all right?* Again I nodded, again I forced a smile. Then I turned and pushed my way back through the crowd, out into the chill, damp evening.

I followed the smell of the sea back to the wharves, avoiding the few soldiers who hadn't given in to the lure of the taverns, and stopping to ask a half-drunk sailor which was the Lower Wharf. A breeze had come up, blowing away the fog at last, and stars glimmered in the sky. A sickle moon lighted the river, making a sparkling moon-trail across the water. I hastened back through the marshes until I reached the willow where our boat was tied. Papa sat there, still alert, with Dickon dozing in his arms.

"I found them!" I said, keeping my voice low. "Jacob, and three others! They say to row to the *Grace Dewe*. Out past the Lower Wharf. I can show you where."

Dickon roused and sat up. "Will my lady mother be there?" he asked eagerly. I shook my head, and his face fell.

"But Master Thaddeus will," I told him. "Do you remember him? Your mother's fool? He loves you well, and he'll take care of you."

His lips trembled. "I want my mother."

"Master Thaddeus will help you," I assured him. "And there are two other men as well, to guard you and keep you safe."

"Will you come, Nell?" he pleaded.

I looked at Papa. I was so very tired. I didn't want to go to France. I wanted to go home, to be with the people I knew, to be safe. But Toby wouldn't be there, and I was beginning to realize that I could never go home again, that I *had* no home. King Richard knew that I had helped Toby to escape. His people would pursue me all my life.

"Your Majesty, I cannot send my daughter to France," Papa said gently. "She has risked her life already. For a young girl to go to a country where she knows no one—it would be the end of her. I sent my son to his death." His voice broke. "I cannot do the same to my daughter."

"No, Papa," I whispered. "It was not your fault." But he turned his head away.

"You have many supporters, Your Majesty," Papa continued, quietly. "They'll care for you and get word to the queen your mother that you are well. She will come to you as soon as she can."

"Will she?" Dickon said. In his voice longing and disbelief battled.

"She will," Papa promised. I didn't know if he spoke the truth or not. He was right about one thing, though: I could not go to France, even to put myself out of King Richard's reach. I couldn't speak French, knew no French people. There was nothing more I could do for Dickon.

We untied the skiff and climbed in, and Papa rowed us back onto the Thames. I tried to keep the location of the Lower Wharf in my mind as I directed him, for we were out too far to see it. "A little to the left, and straight on," I said, hoping I was right. He strained at the oars, the breeze against him now, and at last we saw a shape looming out of the darkness.

"She bears a French flag!" I hissed. "It must be the *Grace Dewe!*"

We rowed right up to the ship, and Papa called up, as loudly as he dared, "Hello the ship!"

A moment later, a face peered over the deck. In the moonlight I could tell that it was one of the men I had seen at the inn, and I breathed a deep sigh of relief. He didn't speak but lowered a rope ladder over the edge, and Papa grabbed the end of it.

I helped Dickon stand in the rocking boat. He threw his arms around me fiercely.

"I shall miss you, Nell," he said. His voice was stronger than I expected. He sounded almost as much a king as a little boy. "I will see you again."

"I know you will, Dickon. I'll be thinking of you always." I kissed him and led him to the ladder, and Papa and I watched him climb, slowly but with certainty, up to the deck. The man helped him over the railing and pulled up the ladder. Dickon looked back down at us as we bobbed in the river, and then he turned away, and we saw him no more.

CHAPTER FIFTEEN

I lost all sense of what happened next. A terrible fever took hold of me, brought on by the horror and despair and fear of what had happened, by the cold in the marshes and the strain of escape.

I remember a few things: Papa rowing and rowing endlessly, looking for a safe place to bring our skiff to land. A dreadful jouncing ride on horseback that seemed to go on for days, Papa's arms about my waist the only thing keeping me in the saddle. Jacob's worried face. The soft voices and black-and-white magpie cowls of nuns. And then, thankfully, quiet.

When I came to myself, I barely knew where or who I was. That was a blessing, it turned out, for I was no longer myself. The nun who had tended me, Sister Catherine, told me that I was Alice Gold, a motherless child who had been sent to the convent at the behest of a wealthy relative. I don't know who chose my new name, but I embraced it. Alice had been my mother's name. I didn't want to be Nell Gould, the butcher's daughter of Westminster, any longer.

It was a long, strange time before I could fully sense the stone walls around me, the crisp linen sheets over me, the calm women who bustled about me. Sister Catherine explained how I had come to the Convent of St. Anne.

"Your father carried you in, what was left of you. You'd nearly burned away from fever. He was sure you'd die."

"Poor Papa," I murmured weakly.

"He left money for your room and board. And there was a young man with him—"

"Jacob."

"Yes, Jacob—I've sent word to him that you're mending. Your father could not give me his own address. Why is that?"

I shook my head against the pillow. Of course—Papa had no address because he could not go home. King Richard's men would know to look for him. I hoped that Jacob, or perhaps Master Caxton, had found a safe place for him.

I spent long, peaceful days indoors, regaining my strength. The sisters brought me invalid's food, and I sipped broth and ate milk toast until I could walk again. And then I walked to the chapel, a beautiful, quiet place where colors from the stained glass danced on the floorboards and the sweet smell of burning candles nearly overwhelmed me.

I prayed for hours each day, until one of the sisters noticed me and helped me to my feet, scolding me for being up and about in my state, for subjecting myself to the chill of the bare floor and the winds of the cloister that linked the nuns' cells and the chapel. I welcomed the discomfort, though, looking for ways to punish myself. Over and over in my head, I played out my actions. I had taken Toby into the Tower. I had insisted on staying when I might have gotten us safely away. Because of me, Toby had died. Why, I raged to myself, was I the one left alive? Why not Toby, innocent and dear? Why not Ned, the true king? I prayed desperately for forgiveness, but I found no consolation.

I had nightmares almost every night, too. Sometimes I would dream I was back in the Garden Tower, in my room, in my bed with Dickon, and I would hear those footsteps again. I wouldn't be able to move, but I knew. I knew what would happen, and I could not stop it. Other times, I would be in Ned's room, and I would see the man with the greasy hair come in, a gleaming knife held high, and I would see him bring it down on the sleeping shapes in the bed. I was there but not there, as you are in a dream, and I could not stop it. But the worst were the dreams where I was in my tower room and it was Toby with me in the big bed, and when the footsteps passed I knew he was safe, and then I'd wake on my narrow convent cot, realizing it wasn't true, my pillow soaked with sweat and tears.

At last, not knowing what to do with me, Sister Catherine sent me to the abbess, a tall, once-beautiful woman whose sharp features contradicted the warmth in her eyes. She sat on a straight chair before a wooden table in a room empty of all other furniture, with a window that looked out over dead November fields down to a winding river. I stood before her dry-eyed, and she asked me what troubled my soul.

"I am a murderer," I said. "I killed my brother."

"I know your history, Alice," she said to me in a deep voice that was at once commanding and comforting. "I know what happened, and I know that you were not at fault. God has forgiven you for the part you played in that drama; why can you not forgive yourself?"

"I *was* at fault," I insisted. "If it had not been for me, my brother would still live."

"God chooses a time to call each of us to him," she reminded me. "If it was your brother's time, he would have gone, whether you were there or not. Do you set yourself to be more important than God?"

That gave me pause, but not for long. I railed, "But why would God want Toby to die? Why would he want to punish me like that?"

The abbess shook her head. "We cannot presume to know His ways. You are not the center of all things, my dear. You are just a part of the whole. If you learn that from all this sorrow and hardship, then you will have learned a lesson that few know."

I began to cry then, and the abbess let me weep, sitting opposite me in silence until I was spent. Then she sent me back to my bare cell, which had nothing in it but a small bed and a wooden box that held a few of my clothes that someone—Jacob, perhaps?—had sent on from Westminster.

· ● ·

Slowly, I began to notice and join in the life of the convent. Indoors, the nuns observed strict silence at most times. I found it a strain not to speak, and mealtimes were especially difficult: the nuns communicated by using hand signs they had devised, each of which I needed to learn. To ask for fish at the table, a sister would wag her hands as if they were a fish's tail; if she wanted milk, she would move her hands as if milking a cow. The vast number of signs, and the near impossibility of the newest sisters interpreting them correctly, led to many silent arguments—soon hands would be flapping all up and down the table, while not a word was spoken. I would sit staring at my spoon, determined not even to smile, but it was wonderful to feel amused. I had been sad for so long.

I had a hard time, too, getting used to the prayer times the sisters observed. We boarders—there were five of us—were expected to pray with the nuns. We rose at six to say Prime, then through the day prayed at Tierce, Sext, None, Vespers, and Compline as well, ending at seven, because it was winter now. That was not all, though. We were awakened by a silent sister around midnight for Matins, and then a few hours later for Lauds. It took me weeks to grow accustomed to the strange, dreaming-while-waking feeling that such broken sleep gave me, but the frequent rousings interfered with my nightmares, and after a time the bad dreams eased.

Aside from meal and prayer times, I wandered through the convent aimlessly. The sisters in the laundry room would wave their reddened hands at me cheerfully; at least they were warm, in their steamy quarters. The kitchen, too, was warm, though the cellaress always chased me out, fearing I'd take food I was not entitled to. If I passed by the library, with its shelves of books and manuscripts, I held my breath and scurried past so I wouldn't smell the delicious scent of paper that I'd loved so in my other life.

In the weaving room, I noticed that the sisters only dyed their wool a dull brown. For some reason, I remembered the recipe from *The Boke of St. Albans* for dyeing fishing line russet, and I wrote it down for the sister in charge: lye and alum, soot and walnut leaves, boiled well together. It would, I thought, make a nicer color for the cloth while still remaining humble, and if they sold it to townspeople, it would fetch a higher price.

But I needed structure, rhythm. I began to work in the winter garden with Sister Catherine. We toiled from twelve to four each day, and my hands grew rough and callused. I welcomed the hard work in the cold, bright air.

As time passed we became friends, for we could talk outside, away from the silence of the convent halls. I had only spoken to boys—Ned, Dickon, Toby—for so long that I'd forgotten how wonderful it was to have a female friend. There were things about me that, though she was a nun, she could understand as a boy could not.

So I confided in her. One afternoon in the garden, trusting her with my secret, I finally told her of my terrible guilt. I'd thought I had no tears left, but the telling made me cry until my eyes swelled and my throat was raw.

She listened with her whole being, as she always did. She already knew some of my tale, having heard me speak in my delirium of what happened, and she did not judge.

"You have done nothing wrong, sweeting," she said to me. "You need only to forgive yourself."

"How? How can I do that?" I asked her, my voice hoarse with weeping. "It's not just what happened to Toby. It's that I was proud. And my pride cost Toby his life."

"Why do you think that?" she demanded, her hands turning soil with practiced economy. "What does your pride have to do with it?"

"Because I was proud, I thought of myself as Ned's equal. I thought I could be his friend. I thought I could help him. Who was I to think such a thing? I was a tradesman's daughter, and he a king!"

Sister Catherine shook her head. "And what of the Good Samaritan, who helped the man who was robbed and beaten on the road to Jericho? Did it matter that the victim was not of the same tribe, that they were not equals? Of course not! What mattered was that he gave aid in a time of great need. You gave the king comfort, and that is a precious thing. My dear, perhaps you are prideful to consider yourself so very important in the workings of the world. But your despair in the face of God's forgiveness is a far more serious sin."

Her words echoed those of the abbess, but I couldn't accept them. I turned back to my work, yanking cabbages fiercely from the cold ground.

Not all of our conversations were so serious. Sister Catherine liked to tell me about her childhood. Her tales of growing up in a manor house near Bath fascinated me. Her family had been wealthy but fell on hard times, so rather than providing a dowry for the youngest of five girls, they sent her to the convent.

"Did you want to come?" I asked.

She shook her head, laughing. "Oh, how I carried on! I screamed and wept and fought for weeks. I actually hit my head so hard against a wall that I fainted! Here, you can still see the scar." She pulled up her wimple and I saw a faint mark on her forehead. "Once I got here, I stayed in my room and didn't speak for six months. I grew so used to my own silence that obeying the rule of silence in the convent didn't bother me anymore. And then . . . I fell in love with the life here."

"Fell in love?"

"I don't know how else to describe it. The prayers, the daily routine, the sights and smells of the chapel, my own faith . . . I feel it all so deeply. I am content." Her smile was faint and faraway, indeed like that of a woman in love. At that moment I envied her very much.

When the season turned and the days began to warm, I had a visitor. Jacob came to the convent door, and the abbess called me into her office to ask if I wanted to see him.

"It is your decision," she said. "You have settled in here well, and if you feel that speaking with him will disturb the peace you have found, you are free to refuse."

"No, I will see him," I said. I longed for word of Papa, and of the outside world. Though I had grown to love the convent—its quiet calm and regularity, the kindness of the sisters—I didn't feel Sister Catherine's contentment. Something in me yearned for the world outside.

Jacob and I sat awkwardly at the table in the convent dining hall, the door wide open, and curious sisters passed by as often as they dared to peek in at him. We seldom had male visitors, and few were as handsome as Jacob had become.

"Your father is well," he told me, leaning across the table. He tried to grasp my hands, but I moved them to my lap. "He lives in the country with my parents now, and butchers for their village. Master Caxton managed to sell his shop for him, so he is comfortable and will be so for life."

I was more than relieved to hear it. I had pictured Papa wasting away from sorrow and fear, but though I knew he must miss Westminster and his friends and neighbors, it was good to hear that he would not have to rely on charity and could still work.

"You've seen him?" I asked, my heart aching.

"Yes, a month or so ago."

"Does he . . . does he blame me?" It was a question that I'd tormented myself with. I hardly dared to ask it.

"Blame you?" Jacob was confused. "For what?"

"For Toby."

"Oh, Nell," Jacob breathed. "No, of course he doesn't. He blames himself, to be sure. He may blame the queen, though I've never heard him say so. But not you. Never you."

I willed myself to believe it. I longed to believe it.

"So King Richard never found him? Never questioned him?"

"He questioned Master Caxton, knowing of your connection,

but Master Caxton cannot be intimidated." I smiled. I knew that well. "I never told Master Caxton where you or your father went, so he didn't have to lie. And of course the king didn't think to question me, a mere journeyman."

"But you are a master now," I noted, seeing his robes. They were fine wool, not the threadbare garments he'd worn as a journeyman.

"I am," he said, pleased that I'd noticed.

"Do you know where the princesses are? Are they safe?" I asked. I'd thought often of Cecily. I missed her.

"They're all well, and at court," Jacob said. I was shocked.

"At court? At *Richard's* court? How can that be?"

Jacob shrugged. "King Richard signed an oath, it appears. The mood has been against him, and the queen—I mean, Dame Grey—made him promise to protect and care for them. He even gave her a pension! Quite a bit of money, if the rumors are true. They all left sanctuary when he signed it."

So Queen Elizabeth was now Dame Grey, called by the name of her first husband. And her daughters attended the king's wife! It was all so strange, and so far away from my life now. But I was glad to hear they were out of sanctuary and unharmed.

"They say that King Richard wants to marry Princess Bess."

My mouth dropped open. "But—but she is his niece! And he is married already—or has Queen Anne died?"

"She is still alive, though she's been ill," Jacob said. "But who knows if it's true?"

I shuddered. Poor Bess! Just as Cecily had said, King Edward's daughters were little more than pawns in the workings of government. I hoped for Bess's sake that Queen Anne would rally.

"I brought you these." Jacob opened his satchel and pulled out a small stack of books. I began to thumb through them, but he motioned me to stop. "Look at them later. I'm afraid your abbess will only give us a little time together." I had to smile—he was quite right.

Jacob took a deep breath. "I don't have my own shop yet, Nell. I still work at the Red Pale, and Master Caxton gives some of the best jobs to me. It's far better work than I could get on my own."

"That's wonderful, Jacob," I said, truly happy for him.

"But Nell . . . I would set up my own shop, if that's what you wanted. If I knew that you . . . well, that in a few years you might consider me. I long for you every day. Every single day. Will you—will you consider me?"

I looked at Jacob's dear, familiar face with a great clarity and a great regret. I could never go back to Westminster, I knew that. I could never settle down and marry Jacob the printer and keep house down the street from where my father's shop had been. Even if King Richard had stopped looking for me, I didn't deserve such a happy life. And my heart was still Ned's, though his beat no longer.

"No," I said gently. "I will not consider you, Jacob."

He winced as if he'd been slapped, and I hated to do that to him. But as his expression changed to sadness, I thought perhaps he understood.

"Then good-bye, Nell," he said. He leaned across the table,

and before I could pull back, he kissed me swiftly. Then he stood and left, and that was a good thing, for if I'd had time to think I might have called him back.

Later that day, I looked over the books Jacob had brought. I could hardly believe it. In the middle of the stack was my little notebook—my book of secrets. I opened it to the first page, then closed it again. No, I could not look at those words, at what I had written when I was such a stupid, thoughtless innocent, when Ned was alive and Toby was alive and I was that other girl, Nell Gould.

Instead, I thumbed through the other books. I was startled to see the authors' names: Margery Kempe. Christine de Pizan. Julian of Norwich, whom the abbess had mentioned more than once as a deeply holy woman. And she had written a book—they had all written books!

I remembered my joy at printing Juliana Berners's book. I hadn't known that all these other women were writers as well.

The last book in the pile was *The Golden Legend*, a collection of stories of saints' lives and sayings that Master Caxton had printed many times over. This copy was a little water-stained, the look of it oddly familiar. As I turned it over and over, I had to catch my breath.

It was surely the same volume we'd had when we were staying in the Tower. Ned's hands had turned these pages, and Toby had touched it too.

I clasped it to my chest, and slept with it under my straw-stuffed pillow that night and every night.

The summer garden began to grow, and I relished the sight of the small green sprouts inching their way toward the sun. I felt myself growing upward toward the warmth in the same way. My pale city skin grew brown and freckled, and I had dirt under my nails. I spent more time on my knees digging weeds than praying. In my free hours I tramped in the fields and lay in the sun down by the river, and I read the books Jacob had brought me.

They were strange and wonderful, each in its own way. Margery Kempe told her own story, that of an ordinary woman, a brewer who had visions of Jesus Christ and traveled on pilgrimage all the way to the holy city of Jerusalem. Christine de Pizan's *Book of the City of Ladies* described an imaginary city where all the famed women of history lived and talked together: Dido, queen of Carthage. Nicostrata, who invented the Latin language. The orator Hortensia. Sappho, the Greek poet. St. Christine, St. Fausta, St. Cecilia. The courageous queens Artemisia and Berenice. And Julian of Norwich wrote of her relationship with God so tenderly that I was deeply moved. Each of them spoke, it seemed, to my heart in their writings. Kempe told me, "Daughter, you have despised yourself, for which reason you will never be despised by God." How did she know this about me? De Pizan reminded me, "A person whose head is bowed and whose eyes are heavy cannot look at the light." And it was true. And Julian of Norwich whispered to me, "All shall be well, and all shall be well, and all manner of things shall be well." This was the hardest for me to believe, but saying the words to myself, with their rhythm of hope, gave me some small comfort.

A messenger arrived that June with a note for me from Master Caxton. In the gentlest words possible, he told me that Papa had died. He died in his sleep, and Jacob's mother found him in the morning when she came to call him to his meal. He had been very ill during the spring, Master Caxton wrote, and had been planning to write to me, but had been too weak to put quill to paper. He had died at peace. He was buried next to Mother, and they would rest together for eternity. There was money in the letter, too—quite a bit of money. I didn't know if it had come from Master Caxton or from Papa.

I couldn't cry when I read the news. I had drained myself of tears during my own illness, and the months after, and I found that I was dry. But I wept inside, where my memories of Papa lived. When I recalled the feel of his rough beard against my cheek or the sound of his laugh, I would have to stop whatever I was doing and wait until the grief that pierced me eased. I had no family now, no one who linked me to my past.

My heart was heavy, but I went on. Prayer and field work lightened my burden. The rhythm of daily life in the convent carried me along, and the seasons passed calmly. Nothing changed in the convent except the weather. Prayers seven times daily, meals at regular hours, work in the garden—each day was nearly the same as the day before. In such quietude I moved gratefully, hoping only for silence and peace.

But war came to us instead.

CHAPTER SIXTEEN

It was late in summer—I had long ago lost track of days—when we heard, as we filed toward the chapel for our predawn prayers, the sounds of metal clashing and horses' hooves outside the convent walls. The sisters ignored the noise, but I, at the end of the line, ducked into a doorway and waited until the others had entered the church.

I ran through the cloister to the outer door and peered out through the peephole. The first light of day showed passing before me a line of soldiers, marching heavy in their armor. They seemed to stretch for miles, and I stood watching for a long time as they passed. At some point Sister Catherine joined me, and we gazed together at the faces of men tired and longing for home, and of boys excited at the prospect of battle, sure they would become heroes and return to their families with tales of great courage and daring.

"Who are they?" I whispered. "Where do they go?"

"They are King Richard's men," Catherine whispered back.

"I heard the abbess talking to the priest. They say there is a challenger to the king. Henry—Henry Tudor, that was his name. I don't know who he is, nor why he would feel the crown should be his, but war is upon us. I fear these men are marching to their deaths."

I shivered, watching them march. Which ones were marked for death? Was it the heavyset man with the red beard, whose sword clanked loudly by his side? Or the two dark-haired boys marching together—brothers by the look of them—too young for beards but old enough for battle?

I wondered if King Richard himself marched in this column. *His* death I could wish for. I could even desire to see it, I thought.

And suddenly I felt that I *must* see it. Perhaps if I witnessed the king's death, it would erase the horrors of Ned's and Toby's from my imagination. Perhaps I would feel some measure of justice.

Quickly, before I could think too hard on it, I lifted the heavy bar from the gate and opened the door.

"Alice!" hissed Sister Catherine. "What are you doing?"

"I'm going to watch the battle," I told her.

The line of soldiers had passed now, and following behind them were people from Bosworth Market, the town nearby. To them, a battle was an amusement—if seen from far enough off.

"No, it's not safe!" Sister Catherine protested.

"I must. Please, don't try to stop me." I slipped through the gate, leaving Sister Catherine staring helplessly after me. I didn't give a thought to the trouble I was making for her by leaving the convent. I only knew that I had to go.

Outside the convent wall, amid the mass of people, there was talking and even gaiety. The men and women—children too!—who surrounded me as I walked looked forward to an afternoon's entertainment, not thinking at all of the men who would die, the families who would be bereaved. I had never seen nor been anywhere near a battle before. I was shocked to see it treated the way a mummers' play or joust would have been in Westminster.

I walked for several miles, to the top of a rise. The land spread out before me, a great field stretching off into the distance. The grain had recently been harvested, so the field was bare and dusty. The sun had risen and was beating down with August heat, and I could feel the perspiration trickle down my back. A heavy woman with a red, shiny face offered me cider, and I took it and drank gratefully.

"Who is this Henry Tudor?" I asked her. Most anyone would have more word of the world than I, safe inside the cloister.

The woman laughed. "He's not King Richard. I'n't that enough?"

Her husband, a fellow maybe half her size, said, "Treasonous woman!" but he spoke with irony. She laughed again and cuffed him on the side of the head, rocking him back on his heels.

"The Tudor is descended from our King Edward the Third, they say," the man told me. I had to think about this for a minute. Edward the Third was Ned's great-great-great-grandfather. So Henry Tudor really had some claim to the throne!

"He's been in France all these long years," the man went on, "just waiting for his chance. He's as much of a right to the throne as King Richard has, in my view. Damn the king for a sneaking, murdering cur!" The wife cuffed her husband again, and he seemed suddenly to see me clearly. "Oh, beg pardon, Sister," he said. "No offense meant, I'm sure."

I looked down at myself to see why he had mistaken me for a nun. I'd forgotten that I wore a scapular over my dress as the sisters all did, to protect my clothes when I worked outside. But it would have been too complicated to explain that I was just a boarder—and I wanted no questions about my identity raised in anyone's mind.

"No offense taken," I assured him. "I am no supporter of King Richard."

"Is anyone?" the wife asked, and they walked away, looking for the best vantage point to view the battle.

I was amazed. I had not known that the people hated King Richard so; I'd been sunk so long in my own thoughts and feelings that I had never considered he might not be accepted as King Edward had been before him. From the sounds of the crowd that surrounded us, though, Richard was roundly despised. I heard reference over and over again to the murder of his nephews, and with each remark, my heart ached.

" 'Twill be God's justice if he's cut down the way he cut down our poor princes!"

"Better a king we don't know than one we know to be a murderous devil!"

"I'll see his lying head stuck up on a pike to avenge those innocents!"

As the morning progressed, I began to regret having come. I had managed my grief, had worked it as a potter might work the clay until it was of a size and shape that I could live with it. There was no talk in the convent of the king and his court to stir up my memories. But now my sadness began to grow until it threatened to overtake me once again. And I knew that my absence would surely make the abbess furious.

I was about to turn back when suddenly a call sounded. In the distance I saw a line of soldiers approaching along the ancient Roman road that led through the field. Henry Tudor's men.

Tudor rode at the head of his soldiers on a fine gray palfrey, and his armor shone in the blazing sun. How hot the troops must be, roasting in their metal casings! The line of soldiers came on and on, and King Richard's men arranged themselves across the field, waiting.

I was suddenly breathless, and I pushed my way out of the press of spectators around me. I scrambled up a small, steep outcropping to a rock plateau where no one else stood.

The crowd hushed, and I could hear the clanking of armor and swords and the neighing of horses as the armies neared each other. A cluster of mounted men stood to the side of King Richard's army, and I noticed one of them, tiny in the distance, astride a white charger.

I knew him immediately for Richard of Gloucester.

He drew my gaze, and I watched him closely as the soldiers

closed ranks. If he raised his eyes, I wondered, would he be able to see me, standing alone on my rock?

Would he know who I was? Would he think, *There is the girl who escaped me?*

The two armies faced each other motionless across the field. To me, far above them and far away, they seemed almost to be toy figures, like the carved chess set Ned and I used to play with. The silence stretched and stretched, and then, with a trumpet blast that rose up until the leaves on the trees trembled, the armies came together.

I shuddered as swords shaved through flesh, horses screamed and fell, and blood began to run, turning the dust to a ghastly red mud. King Richard sat motionless on his horse, watching as I watched.

I thought of the evening long ago when we had both heard King Edward and his queen arguing. I longed to have him look up and meet my eyes as he had that night. Today I wanted him to see me, to know that I was watching. I wanted him to realize that I bore witness—to his evil work, and, perhaps, to his death.

The battle went on and on, and the dust rose and swirled. When the hot wind stirred, I coughed and choked from it and from the metallic, fetid smell of blood and death that it carried to me. The watchers around me grew almost mad with excitement as Henry Tudor's men poured onto the field and King Richard's soldiers died.

"*For Tudor! For Tudor!*" a man next to me shouted, and others took up the cry until our hillside rang with it. *"For Tudor! For Tudor! For Tudor!"*

I kept my sights on King Richard, who stayed unmoving where he was. And then he raised his sword arm and pointed.

There was Henry Tudor astride his gray, a figure of stillness in a whirl of men and swords. King Richard spurred his horse and raced toward his enemy, his men following.

Henry signaled, and then, from the hills across the field, a new stream of soldiers poured into the battle. For long moments I lost sight of both Henry and Richard. Then the sea of horses and men parted, and I clearly saw Richard of Gloucester, his blade swinging. He was bloodied. He was weakening.

I saw his white horse falter.

I saw him fall.

Then I could see him no more.

Most of the townspeople stayed to watch the end of it all, to see one army rout the other from the field, but I left the hillside and walked back to the convent in silence. I had thought I would feel a great relief, even joy, when I knew that King Richard was dead. But I felt nothing.

Henry Tudor was king now. Richard the Usurper was dead.

But so was Ned. And so was my brother, Toby.

CHAPTER SEVENTEEN

Trouble awaited me, though Sister Catherine hadn't revealed where I'd gone until the others had truly begun to fear for me. The abbess lectured me on the selfishness I'd shown by leaving and worrying everyone, but when she saw the misery in my eyes, she took pity on me and only commanded that I scrub the scullery as punishment. And even that went unfinished, because the wounded began staggering up to the convent gate to beg for water, food, and help.

Everyone ministered to them, even ancient Sister Aldetrude, who was nearly blind and spent most of her time sitting on a cushion in the refectory. We had no hospital and little training in physic, but the older sisters were well versed in the use of herbs to ease pain, and were completely undaunted by the ghastly wounds that sent some of the younger nuns scrambling for a pot or bucket to vomit into. Our refectory became a hospital, with beardless boys and gray-haired grandfathers alike writhing on makeshift pallets on the floor.

We bound up limbs spurting blood and hands missing fingers, gave water and comfort to the living and prepared the dead for burial as best we could. It seemed that the stream of wounded would never end. I still could not say how many hours we spent like that, moving from man to man, wiping the brow of one and covering the lifeless face of the next.

Night passed into day and then night again before we stopped. The refectory floor was slippery with blood, and all of us were soaked and sticky with it from head to foot. The smell was sickening, and I fled to my little room to strip off my clothes and try to wash myself. Sister Catherine followed me, and we scrubbed with rough towels and cold water until we were clean enough to bear it. Then we collapsed.

"My God, my God," Sister Catherine murmured. I did not know if it was a curse or a prayer. "How can men do such things to each other?"

"That is what men do," I said wearily.

She shook her head, too exhausted to argue with me. We fell asleep together on my narrow cot, and did not wake for nearly a day.

The whole week was spent nursing, the usual work of the convent pushed aside so we could care for the fallen soldiers. Many more died, and were buried quickly in our cemetery, but some walked or hobbled out on their own, headed back to the towns and villages they hailed from, to tell the story of the Battle of Bosworth to their admiring friends and families. One boy, not more than thirteen or fourteen years old, reminded me just a little of Toby, with his freckled face and bright blue eyes. His name was Martin, and he had a leg wound that healed well. I helped him to fashion a crutch from a tree branch.

"Your mother must be frantic with worry," I said to him as I checked his wound and rebandaged it.

"Aye, I'm sure she is," he said carelessly.

"You should not have gone."

He stared at me with those wide Toby eyes. "But Sister!" he protested. "It was a grand battle—and we won! The wicked King Richard is dead and gone!"

"And why was he wicked?" I asked. But Martin had no answer. It was what he'd been told, and what he believed. And though I knew it to be true, I couldn't celebrate my revenge. Death begat death, and murder led to murder. I wanted no more of it.

When the refectory-hospital was nearly empty, we returned to our daily lives. I couldn't settle back into the convent schedule, though. I was restless and found it hard to empty my mind during prayers or in the garden.

One afternoon I went outside alone to sit in my favorite place, under a tall oak by the river. I brought two books with me: the copy of *The Golden Legend* that Jacob had left for me and my book of secrets.

I thumbed through my little notebook, reading my jottings about the princes and princesses, our games, the royal celebrations and festivals. Had we really once watched a feast that had forty-seven different dishes? Had I actually tossed marbles down the hallways of the privy palace with the royal family? It seemed unbelievable, even grotesque to me now.

Cecily invented a new game today. We took a rush mattress and brought it to the staircase, and then took turns riding it down the stairs. Bess didn't like it because it bumped too much, but oh! it was so much fun! Or it was until Lady Mistress Darcy discovered us.

I read it all, every word. The rush of emotions that reading my descriptions brought was nearly overwhelming, and for a little while I lost myself in the past. For the first time, I tried to recall what it had been like, in that other life. I was someone else now, but I had once been the girl who wrote of those astonishing, beautiful things. How happy I had been—how lucky I had been!

When I had finished, I closed my eyes for a few minutes, remembering. Then I wiped my cheeks of the tears I hadn't even known I'd shed, and reached for *The Golden Legend*. Perhaps I was looking for some saint's words that would help me make sense of all that had happened. I came to a section on St. Edward, King and Martyr, that made me think of Ned. St. Edward had been king of England for only a short time and had been murdered in a dispute over the crown, just like Ned. I flipped through the pages. Then I stopped, shocked.

There were marks on some of the words, above the second letter. The same marks we had used to decipher the queen's message when we were in the Tower. I was certain that this book hadn't been marked when we first got it from Jacob.

I ran back to my room and found a quill and paper, and began writing down the marked words: *Edward—was—murdered*. I caught my breath. Whose message was this? I read the sentence again, and closed my eyes at the ache I felt in my chest.

In a minute I picked up the quill and searched for more marked words. When I was done, I looked at the whole message.

Edward was murdered. Do not suffer sorrow. He was greatly comforted and much loved. Be joyful in your heart.

I read the words over and over, bewildered at first. But gradually it came clear to me that they were Ned's. Who else would have marked them in that way? Ned must have known what would happen, and he had resigned himself to it. Of course he had. He'd studied politics and kingship for years at Ludlow, under his brilliant uncle's tutelage. He knew well how men of power plotted and schemed. All that time I'd thought he was hopeful—the cheerful smiles, the stories we'd made up about running away together—he had only been pretending. He must have marked the words just before that terrible night in the Garden Tower, and given the book to Brackenbury. They were his last message—to me, or to whoever came across them and could figure out the code. And they showed that he knew he was soon to die.

At first, I thought the anguish of knowing this would

crush me. I bent over the note, trying to draw a deep breath. Had it been all for nothing, then? Had I failed even to bring him hope?

But some of the words Ned had marked sounded again in my mind. *He was greatly comforted and much loved.* I hadn't managed to give Ned hope, but perhaps I'd given him comfort. And maybe comfort was enough.

Be joyful in your heart. Be joyful in your heart. I imagined Ned saying it to me. I could almost hear his voice, and my heart unclenched just a little. After a long time, I fell asleep on my cot with the book still in my hand and the words in my head, and I slept without dreams.

In the garden the next afternoon, Sister Catherine turned to me. "And what will you do now, Alice?" she asked.

"What do you mean?"

"You are free. King Richard is dead. There is no more need for you to hide."

I blinked. Hide? I had not thought of my time in the convent as hiding. But to be sure, Sister Catherine was right. I had hidden myself away from everything. I'd wanted to disappear, and I'd had to, when Richard was king. And now, if I chose, I could rejoin the world.

"I wonder . . .," Sister Catherine mused. "Will your Prince Dickon try to regain his throne?"

My eyes widened. "What do you mean?" I asked again.

"He is free now as well. He's hidden in France all this time. Now he will have a choice to make."

"He's still so young," I protested. "If he even lives. He was so sick."

Sister Catherine put a gentle hand on my arm. "Surely he lives. The stories that come out of France all say so. And after your great sacrifice—it is only right that he lives, and lives well."

"My great sacrifice?" I said with some bitterness. "Do you mean Toby?"

"No indeed!" she said. "I mean the time you spent caring for the prince, and for his brother the king. It is because of you that Prince Dickon is alive. Your compassion and courage are the only reason he survived."

This was not the story I had been telling myself. In my version, I had sinned and betrayed, my prideful actions causing the death of my dear brother and my beloved prince. But was mine the right version—the only version? I thought of what the abbess had said to me soon after I first came to St. Anne's: *You are just a part of the whole.* Perhaps she was right. Perhaps I was the part that helped a little boy—the rightful heir to the throne of England—to live.

"Is it true?" I asked Sister Catherine. "Has my life really been spent helping Dickon to live his story?"

"We cannot know that, Alice. Only God knows that."

"But what should I do next?" I pleaded.

"Write what happened," she said. "There is a reason why you know how to read and write. Put your pain on paper. Empty it from your soul and give it to God. Then you will be free to live your *own* story."

I thought again of the days I'd spent printing Juliana Berners's treatise on hunting and fishing. I'd longed to write a book then, knowing that women could do such things. I didn't know if I still wanted that. And yet, something in me longed to put pen to paper again.

"What if someone finds it and reads it?" I asked. What I'd done helping Dickon to escape had been treason when I did it. Was it still treason, with a new king on the throne?

"Who would believe such a tale?" she replied, her round face creased with a kind smile. I took a deep breath.

Be joyful in your heart. For the first time, I thought that maybe I *could* be joyful in my heart again. I wanted to write that tale, pour it out, and then fill the emptiness where once I'd held Ned, where I'd held Toby, with something else. With my own story. A terrible weight was lifting from me. I raised my eyes to Sister Catherine. "I hope Dickon doesn't come back," I said fiercely. "I hope he lives a long and happy life in France, with people who love him."

"And you should as well, my dear," she replied, hugging me. "You must live a long and happy life somewhere, anywhere you choose. With people who love you. And you can choose them too."

"So I can," I said in wonder. It was a strange new idea, that I could decide my own fate.

I could become a nun if that were to be my calling. Or I could leave the convent and settle in a village somewhere, open a shop with the money Master Caxton had sent me. I could marry, have children, write my own treatises and tales. So much freedom, after so little for so long!

It was overwhelming, even frightening. But something in me rose gladly to it.

"So I can," I said again. "And so I will!"

Sister Catherine and I smiled at each other for a long moment. Then, with a single quick glance toward the field where only a few weeks before a king had died and a new king triumphed, we turned back to the garden to work the soil and tend the summer plants.

THE HISTORICAL FACTS (AND SOME RUMORS)

During the reign of Edward IV, his wife, Queen Elizabeth, fled to sanctuary in Westminster, where a butcher named John Gould brought the pregnant queen "half-a-beef and two muttons for each week of her seclusion." Gould was later made butcher to the new prince's household as a reward. Whether he really had a wife or any children is unclear. He probably didn't know William Caxton, but Caxton did have a shop in the sanctuary district outside the abbey, where he printed many of the books included in this story.

Richard, Duke of Gloucester, brother of King Edward IV, usurped the throne after Edward's death in 1483, much as I have described it. He imprisoned his two nephews in the Tower of London, and after August 1483 the boys were never seen again. Most historians believe, sadly, that they were murdered on his orders. There is no proof that either boy survived, though rumor had the younger, Richard of York (Dickon), seen everywhere from France to the household of Sir Thomas More, a famous English intellectual.

King Richard himself died at the Battle of Bosworth Field, where his army clashed with Henry Tudor's in 1485. For centuries his body was lost, but in 2012 a very old skeleton was found beneath a parking lot in Leicester, England. Experts believed it possible that the remains were those of Richard III, and scientists began studies on the body. DNA matching, a curved spine, and evidence of battle wounds confirmed the identification. In 2015 the king was reburied in Leicester Cathedral, 530 years after the battle in which he was killed.

Elizabeth Woodville, Edward IV's queen, retired to a convent in 1487. She was forced to do so after she was suspected of joining in a conspiracy against the new king, Henry VII. King Henry took all her estates and their income from her. He provided her with a pension, though, allowing her to live very comfortably and see her daughters frequently. She died in 1492, possibly of bubonic plague.

The daughters of Elizabeth and Edward had rich and turbulent lives. During the reign of Richard III, rumors spread that he wanted to marry Princess Bess—Elizabeth of York, Edward's oldest daughter—but this has never been proven. After Richard's death, Princess Bess married the new king, Henry Tudor. Her first son, Arthur, died, but her second son became King Henry VIII, one of England's most famous kings.

Princess Cecily married three times. She wed her third husband without King Henry's permission—possibly because it was a marriage of love, not a political alliance. The angry king banished her from court, and she lived quietly until her death at age thirty-eight.

Princess Anne married Thomas Howard, who after her death was accused of treason under King Henry VIII and imprisoned in the Tower of London. He was the uncle of Anne Boleyn and Catherine Howard, both of whom became wives of Henry VIII and both of whom were beheaded.

Princess Catherine married William Courtenay. Their son

Henry was suspected of conspiracy under King Henry VIII and beheaded in 1538.

Finally, Princess Bridget became a nun when she was about thirteen years old. She corresponded with all her sisters; her sister Elizabeth supported her financially once Elizabeth became Henry VII's queen.

Rumors and confusion always surrounded the princes' disappearance, and from time to time, pretenders emerged. In 1486, a nine-year-old boy named Lambert Simnel appeared in Oxford claiming to be Prince Dickon. The tool of English noblemen who disputed King Henry VII's claim to the throne, Simnel was sent to Ireland with his minders to raise an army. There he changed his claim, pretending instead to be the son of George Plantagenet, the murdered Duke of Clarence. His army was defeated by King Henry's in 1497, and the conspirators behind his uprising were executed. Instead of imprisoning Simnel, the king kindly pardoned the child, put him to work in his kitchens, and eventually made him his falconer.

Similarly, in Ireland in 1491, a young Fleming named Perkin Warbeck was mistaken for a nobleman when he was seen wearing his master's fine clothing. Capitalizing on this error, Warbeck allowed himself to be identified as Prince Dickon. Supported by King Edward IV's sister Margaret—the real Dickon's aunt—as well as the kings of Scotland and France and other powerful leaders, the charismatic Warbeck raised a small army and traveled to England. When he and his forces faced

King Henry's massive army, however, Warbeck fled. He was captured, attempted to escape, and was finally hanged in 1499.

But there may be an answer to the princes' ultimate fate. In 1674 King Charles II had some renovation work done on the Tower of London. During excavations, workers uncovered two skeletons, both child-sized. The skeletons were exhumed and examined by a panel of experts. All agreed they were the bones of Edward and Richard, the sons of Edward IV. Early twentieth-century studies on the bones by a professor of anatomy and a dentist determined that one child had a disease of the jaw and gums. A stain on the skull of the older boy led the examiners to suggest that he had probably been suffocated. No DNA studies have ever been done on these bodies, so there is still no definite proof of their identity, but the bones were buried in Westminster Abbey, in an urn with this inscription:

Here lie the relics of Edward V, King of England, and Richard, Duke of York. These brothers being confined in the Tower of London, and there stifled with pillows, were privately and meanly buried, by the order of their perfidious uncle Richard the Usurper.

A NOTE ON EVENTS

Daughter of the White Rose is based on true events that took place in England between 1470 and 1485. But the book is a work of fiction, so there are incidents and characters in it that I invented. Although John Gould, the butcher who aided Queen Elizabeth in her time of need, was a real person, his daughter Nell is my own creation, as is her brother Toby. Jacob the printer's devil is also an invention, though his employer, William Caxton, lived and worked in Westminster, as did Wynkyn de Worde, who took over Caxton's press when he died. In places, I have also altered the timeline slightly to serve the action of the story.

Nell learns to read and write, both in English and in Latin, which is something very few girls would have had the opportunity to do. Some noblewomen and female members of the royal family might have learned Latin from tutors at home, but it was a rarity in medieval England. Women who wanted an education were most likely to achieve it by entering a convent. Though some noblewomen kept diaries or journals as Nell does, this, too, was an unusual practice.

In *Daughter of the White Rose*, Jacob is introduced as an apprentice and later becomes a journeyman. By the end of the story he is a master, though he is still very young. This was generally the path a craftsman would actually take, but an apprenticeship might last for up to ten years, and a worker might be a journeyman for many more years. A journeyman would become a member of the guild, a union of workers in his profession. He would then have to produce a "masterpiece," a work showing remarkable skill, to achieve the title of master. However, because printing was new to England in the 1400s, there was no specific printers' guild. By the mid-1500s, printers had become an important part of the guild called the Worshipful Company of Stationers, but before that, there were no official rules about when printers could become masters.

Prince Richard's (Dickon's) escape is entirely my own invention. No one truly knows what happened to the sons of Edward IV, so history is rife with rumors about their fates. Because figures pretending to be Dickon appeared after the end of the Wars of the Roses, I chose to imagine that he survived. And who knows—maybe he really did!

TIMELINE

September 1422
Henry VI is crowned king of England at age one.

May 1455
Battle of St. Albans, first battle of the Wars of the Roses.

June 1461
Edward IV is crowned king of England.

May 1464
Edward IV marries Elizabeth Woodville.

February 1466
Princess Elizabeth is born.

August 1467
Princess Mary is born.

March 1469
Princess Cecily is born.

October 1470
Henry VI is restored to the throne; Edward IV is exiled to Flanders.

November 1470
Prince Edward is born in sanctuary.

April–May 1471
Edward IV returns to England; Battle of Tewkesbury; Edward IV becomes king again.

May 1471
Henry VI dies in the Tower.

August 1473
Prince Richard is born.

July 1475
Edward IV invades France.

August 1475
Treaty signed between England and France; Princess Elizabeth is betrothed to the dauphin of France.

November 1475
Princess Anne is born.

November 1477
William Caxton publishes the first book in England.

February 1478
George, Duke of Clarence, dies in the Tower of London.

August 1479
Princess Catherine is born.

November 1480
Princess Bridget is born.

May 1482
Princess Mary dies.

January 1483
Princess Elizabeth's betrothal is broken off.

April 1483
Edward IV dies.

July 1483

Richard III is crowned king of England.

July 1483

Edward V and Prince Richard are last seen in the Tower.

August 1485

Henry Tudor wins the Battle of Bosworth Field; the Wars of the Roses end.